Praise for Myra McLarey's *Water from the Well*

"A fresh, new voice after all . . . McLarey's narrative, which spans more than 100 years, flows from description to dialogue and back again without boundaries, in true front-porch fashion, its eddies and repetitions have the hypnotic effect of chant. . . . [Those] who thrill when emotional rewards come on schedule, if often in unexpected ways, will find *Water from the Well* exactly their Mason jar of ice sun-tea."
—Michael Harris, *Los Angeles Times*

"In *Water from the Well*, the chaotic is returned to again and again as a source of revelation, of truths at once inexplicable and resonant with meaning. . . . Poetic and magical."
—Ann Cobb, *The Boston Book Review*

"Boldly idiosyncratic and folksy."
—Richard Bausch, *The New York Times Book Review*

"God is in the details, and the details in these stories glow with the affectionate attention of an Arkansas Brueghel."
—Patrick Murphy, *Dallas Morning Star*

"A lyrical first novel that skillfully weaves a glowing, richly textured tapestry that captures the warp and weft of a time and place with exquisite humanity. . . . Complicated characters not easily forgotten, and prose both elegant and original: a satisfying draw from the wells of this promising new writer's imagination."
—*Kirkus Reviews*

"McLarey proves that you can go home again in this lyrical novel. . . . A fine read for those who enjoy being immersed in a rich torrent of language."
—*Publishers Weekly*

"By the time you finish, you'll have soaked up a century's worth of porch stories, and you'll feel that you've tasted the peas and seen the sunsets as well."
—Anne Marie Donahue, *The Boston Phoenix*

"A tour de force, a seamless patchwork . . . some passages are simply breathtaking in their poetic and musical movement."
—Janet St. John, *Booklist*

"*Water from the Well* is a complex, lovely book. . . . The cadences of the text's language, the rhythms of spoken words are brilliant."
—Heddy-Dale Matthias, *Jackson Clarion Ledger*

"[I]t is brilliant and quick and crackles with the imagination and wit of its author and characters."
—Megan Jones, *The Commercial Appeal*

"*Water from the Well* is storytelling at its very finest. Lyrical and moving, it is a source of delight that never runs dry. Myra McLarey's debut is a cause for celebration."
—Jill McCorkle

"*Water from the Well* is strong and poetic. This book will move you."
—Kaye Gibbons, author of *Charms for Easy Life*

Water from the Well

===

Myra McLarey

Scribner Paperback Fiction
Published by Simon & Schuster

SCRIBNER PAPERBACK FICTION
Simon & Schuster Inc.
Rockefeller Center
1230 Avenue of the Americas
New York, NY 10020

First Scribner Paperback Fiction edition 1996

SCRIBNER PAPERBACK FICTION and design are trademarks of Simon & Schuster Inc.

Designed by Laura Hammond Hough
Manufactured in the United States of America

1 3 5 7 9 10 8 6 4 2

The Library of Congress Cataloging-in Publication Data
McLarey, Myra.
Water from the well / by Myra McLarey.—1st Scribner Paperback Fiction ed.
p.   cm.
1. Arkansas—History—Fiction. 2. Community life—Fiction. I. Title.
PS3563.C38355W37   1996
813'.54—dc20   96-8226
CIP

ISBN 0-684-83097-3

In memory of
Charles McLarey, my dad
Nellie Peterson, my sister
Don McLarey, my brother
Corliss Archer Lamb, my niece

━━━━━━━━━

For my daughter, Kristina,
aka TJ

Acknowledgments

I would like to acknowledge some of the people who helped me make this journey into my imagination.

Larry Benn, Aretha Black, Rita Goldberg, and Robbie Jean Walker read the manuscript and offered valuable criticism. Mary Madearis generously shared her local knowledge of southwest Arkansas history and my sister Charlene shared her knowledge of Arkansas flora.

My students at Harvard Extension were a continual source of suggestions and encouragement as I struggled with revisions. Amy Ryan was remarkable in the daunting task of copyediting. Linda

Weeks, Nancy Anderson, and Sarah King urged me on. Ann Darby, Jill McCorkle, and Richard Marius gave timely advice. And the MacDowell Colony gave the glorious gift of time and place.

I am especially thankful to Elisabeth Schmitz, to my agent, Leigh Feldman, and to my editor, Anton Mueller, who made it all possible.

Thanks, too, to my childhood friends, especially Sue, Will (Pee Wee), Ima, Nub, Buddy, and my cousins Peggy and McElroy, who keep the home fires burning. And to my nephews, Brady and Bruce, for always believing I can do anything I set my mind to. My gratitude goes to Pat Steenland for her special gift, and to John Olden (born 1892) for his special friendship.

Most of all, I am grateful to my mother and to my late father for filling our home with music and laughter and stories—and love.

My love and appreciation, always, to Steven Prati, my trusted critic, my best friend, and my partner in life.

Jesus gave her water
    that was not from the well
Gave her living water
    and sent her forth to tell
She went away singing
    and came back bringing
Others for the water
    that was not from the well.

Old Spiritual

Contents

Water from the Well

1

Red Sky at Night

*When it is evening, ye say, It will be fair
weather: for the sky is red.*

Matthew 16:2

APRIL 2, 1919

On the afternoon of April 2, 1919, in Sugars
Spring, Arkansas, the Sugars Spring men's
baseball team boasting three of the best hitters and
the very best pitcher in Hampstead or Harwell
County played the coloreds of Chickenham. Just for
practice of course, since the Hope Cougars, not
wishing to blemish their record, sent word by the
mail carrier that they were down with the fever.
They laid out the diamond in Amos Henry's cow
pasture as they didn't want to scratch and scar
their new field on the ridge between the school
and the Baptist church. And they didn't want to
play in Chickenham—although Lincoln Bradley,

who owned the Chickenham store and an automobile, told them they was most assuredly welcome to—because somehow it didn't set right being hosted by coloreds. So they settled on Amos Henry's cow pasture in the valley which was the last white house—if you didn't count the Ardis Young shacks—before getting into Chickenham, which the coloreds called Bethel, but which was part of Sugars Spring governmentwise and townshipwise.

The day had dawned cold with a starched white sky, and Jack Frost made an unusually late appearance, sparing the ridge but spewing a mist of ice crystals on most everything in the valley. Cora Emery—as she was still called even though she had been Cora McRae ever since she married James McRae shortly after coming to Sugars Spring from her home in Maine nearly twenty years ago—had risen in the half dark, pulling coveralls over her thin wool gown, and poured water on her jonquils, now in full bloom, yellow as a banty egg yolk, and on her irises, just coming into bloom, and spewed with a thin spray of frozen crystal, so they would escape the burn of the gold spring sun that by afternoon had the men on the Sugars Spring team shedding their flannel shirts and rolling the sleeves of their undershirts above their elbows.

David Ben Sugars, who had come back from the war totally intact, even went so far as to strip naked—to the waist—causing the young girls watching to titter, and causing the women to look down at the ground or at each other, pretending not to notice how finely sculpted his body was, bronzed even this early in the year and gleaming with sweat in the heavy air that had fallen on the valley by the time the game got under way.

Then Mr. Davis Huff, a deacon at the Baptist Sugars Spring Church, quietly called David Ben aside and asked him if he didn't think it a mite improper to be in a state of such undress with womenfolk around. David Ben said Mr. Davis Huff was surely right and he had plumb forgot his manners, so he put on his undershirt and rolled up the sleeves. But he still looked naked somehow.

David Ben hit two home runs, one with nobody on, and another with the bases loaded. Then he rolled down the sleeves of his undershirt, put on his brown and white checkered shirt, whacked his cap against his thigh sending out a puff of red dust—fine as gunpowder—and excused himself as he had to drive his mother to her ailing sister's in Hope.

May Ellen Huntley in her grass green dress moved out from the shade of the catawba tree where she watched the game alone—like a hunter stalking a five-point buck—and stepped in front of David Ben as he passed. She batted her eyes and said David Ben, I'd surely like to take a little drive with you sometime in that brand spanking new Model A of yours.

David Ben, looking like a jackrabbit caught in

an automobile's lights, toed the dirt and said surely. Then he stepped around her and walked past the women and the girls, nodding his head to the women. Miz Abigail Huff sighed and said he sure would be one fine catch if his mama would make him grow up and if he could escape snares of the likes of May Ellen who had already led many, young and old alike, to their damnation. And one of the women said, not to mention that May Ellen had utterly destroyed the spirit of her dear father who was a fine man and good minister even if he was a Methodist. And a woman with a faded bonnet said no doubt only his belief that he could by some miracle redeem May Ellen coupled with May Ellen's strong resemblance to her dear, departed mother prevented him from casting his daughter out into the world where she belonged. Miz Abigail Huff said I've said the same thing myself. She said Reverend Huntley must find himself saying just like in the Bible *alas my daughter thou hast brought me low*. The women all nodded their heads in agreement and one of them thanked God that the Lord had been merciful in not letting May Ellen's mama live to see her daughter behave like the daughters of Sodom.

Most of the Sugars Spring team got hits and at the end of the third inning, the score was twenty-one to nothing—not much of a contest, but since school was turned out for planting and most of the farmers, after waiting out the wet boll weevil weather of early March, had finished getting their crops in the day before, there was an air of jollity about it.

Hoss Richards, one of the fielders and a real black one, black as shoe polish, kept hollering at the top of his lungs, I gots it, I gots it, don't nobody gets in my way, I gots this one. Then the ball, each time, slid through his glove like quicksilver. And Cabbage Tramble, whose real name was Isaiah, kept skidding on his behind just as he was about to scoop up a grounder, sending up a trail of red dust.

Little Abe Tramble, the pitcher, who was at least six foot three, threw two zinger strikes to a Sugars Spring batter, then threw the next four so wild that not even a catcher for the St. Louis Cardinals could have caught them much less Rooster McElroy, their catcher, who must have been all of five foot two. The balls went sailing over his jumping height and each time Rooster hollered at Little Abe calling him a dumb turkey and other names that sounded like gibberish.

The women of Sugars Spring, sitting under the magnolia tree on chinkapin benches that Amos Henry had brought out from his barn, had supper to see to so they gathered to leave. The young girls in pigtails and long finger-wound curls and starched cambric dresses said aw Ma can't we stay longer, and the women said not to whine, not to complain, as that would get them nowhere in life. So by the start of the fourth inning the only

women still under the magnolia tree were Cora
Emery McRae, a widow and a Yankee, and May
Ellen Huntley, the pretty daughter of the Methodist minister, who did what they damned well
pleased. And Isannah Sanders, who stayed because
her husband, the Baptist minister and the backup
third baseman, a man old enough to be her father,
loved her so much he couldn't bear for her to be
out of his sight. And whose red hair sliding out
from her gingham bonnet burned the eyes of the
players in the field.

Colored women with homespun dresses and
kerchief-covered heads—women so old their bones
creaked as loud as the door hinges on the Bethel
Baptist Tabernacle Church—sat on stumps and up-
turned wooden buckets under the stand of cottonwoods out in left field, a bevy of children,
barefooted and dressed in faded oversized clothes,
fluttering around them. Their laughter pelting
across the field prompted Miz Abigail Huff, as she
led the women up the slanted rose-colored road
toward town proper, to say she had to allow that
coloreds got more enjoyment out of life than
whites and that maybe it was indeed a blessing to be
simple.

This would not have been a story to be telling
years later if Samuel Daniel McElroy, Rooster's
cousin from Hayden's Landing, had not driven by
in a mule-drawn wagon on the way to Pleasant Gilbert's store to pick up a gasket Mr. Ernest Stone

Junior had ordered for his truck. Samuel Daniel brought the mule to a halt in the middle of the road and called Rooster who was just stepping up to bat to ask him if he wanted a day or two of work cutting barrel heading in Saline bottom. And Rooster said sure as shootin' he did. Then Rooster asked Samuel Daniel if he wadn' at least gonna have a time at bat. Samuel Daniel said he wadn' interested in playing a clown and a fool such as what Rooster and Abe and the rest of 'em be doin'. And Rooster said he supposed Sammy Dan had the bodacity to hit the ball clear to burning hell and back. And Samuel Daniel said he would just this once.

And with that, Samuel Daniel McElroy climbed down off his wagon, told his mule to stay put, took the bat from Rooster's hands, kept his eyes to the ground to avoid the eyes of any white women who might be still around, and ambled to home plate which was a pink-flowered flour sack filled with sand from Amos Henry's white-sand quarry that marked the boundary in right field.

Red Cummings, who Sugars Spring claimed was the best pitcher west of the Mississippi and east of Red River, took one look at this tall young man—skinny as a stray dog with shoulders as wide as Red River and eyes as sleepy looking as a Saturday night drunk's—and decided he'd have hisself a little fun. Red turned his head to the left, shot a mouthful of spit and tobacco to the ground with the force of a bullet and said now that we got Sammy

Dan the great mule trainer up here, let's make it worth sump'n. You manage to get a hit off what I'm gonna throw at you Sammy Dan and we'll declare you Chickenham boys the winner. That all right with y'all? Red gave a sweeping look to his team in the pasture. No one disagreed.

That all right with you Sammy Dan? Red asked with a smile that turned up the left corner of his mouth but left the right corner sitting there. Samuel Daniel McElroy, who carried another name for himself inside his head, didn't say a word, didn't even nod his head. Instead he wiped his forehead—dark and wet looking as molasses—wiped it with the back side of his hand, looked Red Cummings smack dab head on in the eyes with eyes no longer carrying the look of sleep, eyes wide open as a deer's, eyes so black they were purple, for just one second before they eased almost shut again.

Everything seemed to come to a standstill. The colored women under the cottonwood trees quit laughing, and the children grabbed pieces of the old women's dresses and twisted them tight around their hands, tiny and dark as acorns, or buckeyes, or walnuts.

The women parading up the road toward town proper were at least a hundred yards away when they heard the stillness and stopped and turned around. Miz Abigail Huff shifted her slate-colored umbrella to her left shoulder signifying she would stand there in the middle of the rose-colored road to watch. The other women put their hands to their bonnets to extend their view. The girls said what's happening Ma. And the women not knowing the answer said be silent for just one minute please.

The small boys standing around the water bucket quit their game of splash and the smallest one put his hand in his pocket hoping to keep his pond frog, who often croaked at awkward times, quiet.

The men out in the field were thankful their backs were to the sun. It wouldn' do for a nigger like Sammy Dan McElroy to get a lucky hit because they were blinded by the sun that was so bright it was white. Buckner Rose, the first baseman and veteran member of the team, found himself asking the Lord to let Sammy Dan ground out to him. He wanted a chance to tell his friend Ernest Stone Junior, that nigger you say can outwork ten of us couldn't hit no futher than first base—an old codger like me put him out.

Floyd Dillard, the second baseman, already had his mind on paying an after-dark call to May Ellen Huntley whose sashaying, he surmised, was intended more for him than for anyone else. And as his intended—a girl with a well-to-do father and a thin line for a mouth—was visiting cousins in Mineral Springs, there'd be no call to explain his whereabouts.

William Burl Cane, the third baseman, who seemed bound and determined to end up sorry even though he came from a good and respectable and relatively well-off family, but who could make a car engine purr, who could split a dogwood leaf with a bullet, who could stop any ball that came his way and place it in the middle of Buckner Rose's glove before you could draw in air for a sneeze, wasn't even thinking about Samuel Daniel, was thinking instead of Delie Turner the colored woman with glossy hair and skin the color of pecans.

If this were a made-up story, Red Cummings would pitch five times, the tension building up and hanging in the air so you could see it and give it a color. But as it happened, the first ball, Red's special, laden with spit and tobacco juice, zigzagged its way to home plate. Just as it reached the pink-flowered flour sack, it curved out like a purple martin changing direction and any real ballplayer would have known it was outside by a mile and let it go by.

But Samuel Daniel reached for it with what seemed like the slow easy stroke of a man taking a leisurely stretch upon rising the day after the crops are in—sending the ball heavenward, directly over Red Cummings, over Floyd Dillard, over the center fielder, over Amos's cow Mischief, heavy with calf, over the barbwire fence that separated Amos's pasture from Ervin Robertson's, over Ervin Robertson's coffee-colored cow pond and into the grove of persimmon trees that provided shade for Ervin's treasured Guernsey bull.

Sammy Dan ran around the bases, not looking

at Buckner Rose, or Floyd Dillard, or William Burl Cane, or even the catcher whose name no one lays claim to remember since Sammy Dan—not looking up, stretching his legs out to giant strides and swinging his elbows forward and back with the precision of a machine—plowed into him, the catcher, who stood on the pink-flowered flour sack in the quaint notion that the ball might miraculously return from the distant persimmon grove, plowed into him, knocking out the catcher's breath and a front tooth.

Sammy Dan might have redeemed himself, might have alibied himself somewhat had he picked up the catcher and told him how very, mighty, even powerful sorry he was. But he didn't. He simply ceased running, dropped his wide shoulders down ever so slightly, walked at a mule's pace over to Rooster, told him to be at the logging camp by sunup, climbed onto the wagon and made a soft click-click sound to his mule who lumbered on down the road.

The women, some of them with parasols, stood like wax statues in the middle of the road until Sammy Dan got so close they stepped aside to permit him to pass although they probably shouldn't have been so gracious. Sammy Dan kept his eyes on the mule, the mule whose greased neck had attracted enough of the floating dust to turn it the color of cinnamon. The girls said goodness Ma, what's the name of that one, he is so strong. And the mothers said don't you ever, *ever* in all your born

days let your father hear you say that. Don't you
ever even *think* that.

    May Ellen Huntley caught a ride home to the
parsonage with Floyd Dillard who jumped out, ran
around his Model T, opened the door for her, ran
his eyes up and down her grass green dress, and said
she sure was a sight and that he spected he'd probably come scratching on her window screen sometime around midnight. May Ellen flashed her white
smile and with a voice as sweet as a peach but with
eyes looking cold and hard as sapphires said she
spected he just better not. Then she whipped
around and walked up the gumwood sidewalk to
the parsonage.
    Cora Emery McRae, having carried out her
evening chores of laying out hay for her cows, picking the hen eggs, feeding the chickens and wiring the
coop door to secure them for the night, sat on her
front porch steps, the steps of the small white house
her husband James had built and that they had
moved into on their wedding day, sat eating her
supper of cornbread crumbled into a glass of buttermilk, watching her azalea bush soften from crimson
to pink as the sun faded and the sky splattered with
colors in the last light of day, sat missing her husband who had died three years earlier but to Cora
Emery it seemed like yesterday. And a lifetime.
    Cora Emery sat thinking she was glad the night

was warm, sat thinking why was it that of all the things she would need to say to her husband if she could only have him back for just a few minutes tonight, she'd probably find herself telling him about such a silly thing as a baseball game and about Samuel Daniel McElroy, a colored man she knew only by sight but who was the grandson-in-law of Rebekah Sarah, the old, old colored woman who had befriended her, telling him about the sheer beauty of a baseball spinning first, then soaring, like a bird, like that martin across the field from her house, then floating—it had seemed—through the air until it alighted in Ervin Robertson's pasture.

She probably wouldn't tell him about seeing David Ben naked to the waist at the game that day, his skin a rich and glowing bronze giving credence to the story that his great-great-grandmother or some other ancestor was a full-blooded Cherokee. Seeing him stripped of his shirt for those few minutes at the game made Cora Emery realize why women turned their heads or did not turn their heads when he walked by, in much the same way they turned their heads or did not turn their heads when Samuel Daniel McElroy, the colored man with skin the color of walnuts or molasses, walked by on his way to and from the pink-flowered flour sack that was home plate.

Surely James, whose laugh was the first thing she loved about him—no doubt because it balanced the taciturn nature of her Finnish blood that came

as natural to her as the cold winters came to the
Maine village that she still thought of as home, the
Finnish blood that separated her from all of those
about her—surely he would laugh at Red Cummings' face turning crimson in shame. He sure
would have got a kick out of that one she said. First
to herself and then out loud. And then she smiled at
the game and at herself for thinking thoughts that
only a spring chicken should think and for talking
out loud to the sky, or to the azalea bush, and
missed her husband some more.

Isannah Sanders walked home with her husband, caught up in a silence as heavy between them
as the weight of their sleeping child in her husband's
arms. After supper and after Baby William was once
more asleep, Isannah Sanders sat at her dresser in
her muslin nightgown and brushed her hair, red as a
sunset and flowing below her waist, brushed her
hair with her fine brush of polished mahogany,
shiny and dark like the skin of that Samuel Daniel
McElroy.

That sure was a sight to behold she said, thinking to only think it, as the brush slid slow and
dreamlike down her hair, red as fire, and her husband's eyes flared at her and he said what and she
said seeing a ball hit so far, and he said she should
think on better things, he said she was still a child
in too many ways, he said it was time she grew

up, he said she was a mother now, and the wife of a minister.

He got out the Bible and—for their nightly reading—read from Proverbs about a woman whose price was far above rubies.

The husbands sat at the supper tables and ate a plate or two of potatoes, the last of the canned string beans, a jar of pickled peaches, several slabs of smoked ham. They said that nigger look up when he passed you today? Then they went out to their barns and jabbed pitchforks into the hay.

Later in the privacy of the bedrooms, when they were sure their children were asleep, the husbands turned to the wives who may or may not have been asleep, and raising their nightshirts, they yanked their wives' gowns up to their waists, jerked down pantaloons and rammed themselves—rougher than usual—into soft white flesh.

Or they turned their backs and feigned sleep when their wives lifted the quilts, climbed into bed and moved their bodies taut up against the husbands' backs. The husbands listened to the tremor in their wives' breathing. They smelled the rose water, the lilac water the wives had sprinkled in their hair, smelled the talc the wives had dusted on their shoulders. But the husbands did not wake up.

The girls, some still in pigtails although they were in the bloom of womanhood, having recited their prayers, lay on their feather beds looking at the skeletons of the black trees against a sky that had turned from pink to red to violet and now was clean and almost starless, lit by an orange moon. They pulled their braids or twisted their curls around their fingers or tugged at the ruffle of their white nightdresses—iridescent with the moon's touch—and thought of David Ben Sugars and tried not to think how his body might feel, soaped clean of sweat but still warm from the sun, crawling in between clean, freshly starched sun-bleached sheets to lie beside them and twist their hair with his strong brown fingers and gaze with them out the window onto the fields ripe with seed, gaze out on the sagging barns and the soft-lit houses on the other side of this horseshoe ridge. And the black trees under the orange moon.

They tried to cast out the image of that colored man with wide shoulders and skin dark and rich as rosewood, sending a ball into the firmament—higher than they had seen any birds fly, even the winter geese heading for Mossy Lake and then on to Louisiana. They tried to erase the image of a nigger bounding with the grace of a deer around the flour sack bases in Mr. Amos Henry's pasture.

They got out of bed and got down on their knees for yet a second prayer that night, their knees feeling the early April air slithering through the planked floor, air carrying the bite of winter but at the same time perfumed with spring—jonquil and locust and dogwood and magnolia and jasmine. In spite of the draft slipping through their gowns, in spite of the discomfort of the hard floor pressing against their knees, they stayed there, kneeling, needing to pray but not knowing how to name their sin.

So they asked God please not to let them turn out like May Ellen.

David Ben Sugars, as on so many nights lately, left home shortly after supper, left at the beginning of the pink and lonely time of the evening, left in the new Model A his folks had bought for him when he came home from the war, left to go to Hope to play pitch with his war buddies, play until it was after midnight and they were so tired they didn't talk or think about what did or did not happen to them over there, except to talk or think about what they did with the French women even if it did not happen. And sometimes they drank some home brew and at those times they played until the sun came up, until it was no longer night.

On this April evening though, David Ben drove by the parsonage on his way to play cards, slowing down as usual when he passed any house so as not to throw whirlwinds of red dust into the air, whirlwinds that looked like tiny red cyclones, whirlwinds of red dust that found their way into houses or settled on clothes hanging on lines of wire or wooden fences.

Passing the parsonage, he could not help but

see May Ellen Huntley still in her grass green dress, but it seemed to him it was somewhat lower at the shoulders than earlier in the day when she had left him stammering for something to say, could not help but see her sitting on the glider in the front yard of the parsonage.

May Ellen saw him as well and threw a smile and kept on swinging. Even though it was too late for her blue eyes to catch the sun, he remembered them anyway, and remembered how she'd stepped in front of him as he left the game that afternoon to go fetch his mama and carry her to Hope, remembered the smell of violet water that might have come from the violets under her feet but he was sure came from her shoulders, shoulders white as milk. Even though he was driving slow for the sake of the dust, he drove on by the parsonage, by May Ellen Huntley in the glider, drove on by, all the while remembering she had asked him to take her for a drive sometime, remembering again the smell of her shoulders or the violets on the ground. He didn't remember putting his foot on the brake to bring the car to an almost stop, and then to a stop. But finding himself stopped in the middle of the road with soft flutters of red dust finding their way back to the road, he sat there, in his black and polished car, some feet down the road from the parsonage.

But he knew he didn't have to look back. She would be there soon with her smile and her blue eyes and her grass green dress pulled, now, off her shoulders, her shoulders white as the nightgown hanging from the parsonage clothesline even though it might have been dry hours ago. Shoulders that smelled, he was sure, of violets.

Down in Bethel which the whites called Chickenham, Rooster McElroy got pie-eyed on Melvina's whiskey barrel drippings and bragged all night to his children about how they kicked the tar out of them peckerwoods. And his wife said Rooster, you talk like that in daylight, you talk like that when you working with white folks. I'll end up a widow before I'm thirty. And Rooster said don't trouble yourself over that, this old Chickenham Rooster wadn' born yesterday. Then Rooster put his head down on the harvest table between the gravy skillet and his bottle of moonshine, clear as spring water, and slept.

Rooster was asleep by the time David Ben Sugars drove by his house to Garfish Landing which the coloreds call Weaver's Landing, since it was actually on Rebekah Sarah Weaver's land, and where her granddaughter Delie Turner's house backed up against the swamp. In fact, when David Ben's A Model crawled down the trail that passed for road to the landing, he had seen William Burl Cane's truck, looking spit-shined on top where it hadn't been dusted by the road, in front of Delie Turner's house.

David Ben had brought her there because he knew that was where his buddies brought girls like May Ellen Huntley. He sat there wondering what to say as he watched the bank of red lift and fan out around the wild pecan tree between his car and the sunset and thought how the colored woman Delie Turner's skin glowed like pecans as he had sat on the porch of Pleasant Gilbert's store and watched her stride by in the last gleam of light.

He watched the solid red bank thin and fan out, rising above the cypress trees, fan out to cover half the sky, reminding him for just a moment of the red hair of Isannah Sanders, the Baptist preacher's wife, or reminding him of how it might look if she ever left it uncovered and let the wind catch it.

Then May Ellen Huntley lay down across him, her body snuggled between his chest and the steering wheel. She took his face in her hands, and pulled him toward her. Soon the only red he saw was her lips. When he finally looked up again, it was already night, the moon threading its light through the trees surrounding him, and instead of red, he was surrounded by a haze of green—May Ellen's grass green dress, the feathery arms of the cypress trees. The moss green waters of the swamp.

At Delie Turner's house which backed up against the swamp, William Burl Cane sat at Delie's sweetgum table with her sons and drank Melvina's corn whiskey. He ate the squirrel stew Delie had prepared while she rubbed Crazy Sadie's ointment of lard and spirits of turpentine onto Baby Girl's chest and suckled her to sleep. When her sons had their fill, they took some string and went outside to catch the last bit of day, and to catch June bugs and tie strings on their legs for a June bug race. Delie sat down at the table, sat on the bench next to William Burl after he patted it and said come here woman and get you some stew.

And as she ate, William Burl reached across her shoulders and began rubbing her ear. And as she ate, William Burl put his mouth to her other ear and began to nibble, sliding his mouth down her neck. And then Delie gave up trying to eat, sighed and put down her spoon. She reached under the table, reached and found the button on William Burl's trousers, unbuttoned his trousers button by button and then her long, slender fingers found what she was looking for. William Burl Cane groaned and put his hand on Delie's skirt of faded cornflowers, moving his hand down until he reached the spot just above her legs and he moved his hand in small circles over the faded flowers and she moved her hand up and down on him, then the moment when she almost lost her breath and began to moan softly and he said Jesus, God, almighty, damn—at least twice.

After Delie had washed the supper dishes, after she checked on Baby Girl who was tossing and turning in fitful sleep, after she had wiped her sons' faces

and feet with a washrag and told them not to leave
their room, not to even get off their pallets or she'd
blister their behinds, she sat on her bed, sat by William Burl Cane, who was by now sleeping even
though it wasn't fully dark, sleeping from tiredness,
or drink, or pleasure.

She looked at him for a spell. He was good-
looking for a white man. He had dark curls, and
his eyes shaded from horse-apple green to gray
depending on the light. This was the first time ever
he had deigned to stay the night. She wondered
what this meant if anything. She wondered if he
would ever come to her without a bottle of whiskey
in his hand. She remembered the first time he came
to her, dangling three big buffalo fish in one hand,
and a jug of what William Burl called Melvina's
Magic in the other. Came to her the first time when
she was big with the child that was Baby Girl.

Tonight he had come with three squirrels instead of the fish. But in the other hand, jammed
against the jar of whiskey, were some chiggerweeds,
and a few early roses he had swiped from the wild
bushes in Safronia Grant's yard. Delie wondered if
this, too, was love. And if this, too, was something
she needed forgiveness for.

Delie lay there looking past William Burl Cane,
looking out the window, watching the lightning
bugs get brighter as the red sky gathered behind the
tall trees of Mossy Lake, gathered behind the Bethel
Baptist Tabernacle Church where Delie went on

Sundays and prayed for forgiveness for sinning, and for loving, and for loving both the sin and the sinner—watching the lightning bugs get brighter as the red sky gathered behind the swamp and behind the church and then disappeared into darkness.

Finding no sleep in the darkness either, Delie sat up, lifted her gown above her legs and with the quietness of a shadow, straddled William Burl the way as a girl she had straddled her pony. And in the moonlight that was now streaming through her window, she drew her gown over her head, and sat there, her face lifted toward the window, her face caught in the light the moon was casting, it seemed, on her and her alone. Sat there feeling the moon had fastened its beam on her glossy hair, on her skin the color of pecans, filling her with a power she could not name and could not refuse.

She arched her back the reverse of a cat, letting the moon hold her in its spell. Or else holding the moon in her spell. She looked down at William Burl Cane and whispered forgive me, to him and to those she needed—and would again need—to ask forgiveness of but would not.

She looked at him until he was no longer William Burl Cane, until his eyes when they opened would no longer be horse-apple green. She leaned down and one more time whispered softly and earnestly, forgive me.

Then she ran her tongue, firm and soft and warm and gently moist, ran it round and round in

the ear of the man who was no longer William Burl
Cane. She felt him stir beneath her. She leaned
down even more so that her nipples brushed against
his. And now he had grown hard. She raised up and
then eased down over his hardness just as he opened
his eyes, eyes so dark they were purple, opened his
eyes and said Jesus, Delie, why you doin' this to me,
tormenting me even in my dreams, burnin' my body
and my soul.

But Delie didn't say anything, instead she sat
up, threw back her shoulders and locked her eyes
on this man she had conjured not only in her
mind but in the flesh. And his eyes, so black they
were purple, drank in Delie Turner, her eyes brim-
ming, beads dropping from her nipples, nipples
dark as plums. He reached out to her, reached out
with his long arms, arms that in the moonlight
looked like polished mahogany, reached with his
long dark fingers, touched her wet eyes and brought
his fingers to his tongue, reached and touched her
nipples dark as plums, but dropping beads like
pearls, and brought the pearls to his lips. He drank
in her smile, a smile he had never seen on her before.

But he did not smile back. Instead he said
may God in Heaven forgive me, as he reached with
his arms the color of mahogany or rosewood
and clasped Delie's hair, incandescent in the moon's
light, reached and pulled her down to him, pulled
her by her hair toward him, and with her back arching like a cat, he kissed her, kissed her until she cried

and he moaned. They tossed until they became tangled in the top sheet, tossing still until both of them—all of them—hollered Jesus, Jesus, Jesus but they tried not to say it aloud so it came out as a muffled scream.

William Burl lay there, spent, pulled her glossy hair to rest on his chest and said God almighty Delie, what in tarnation is this spell you've cast on me? Delie didn't say anything because she knew it had no name.

The muffled scream woke her sons in the other room who pulled their quilt over their heads and pretended to be asleep. It woke Baby Girl who started to cry. Delie untangled herself from the sheet and from William Burl, went in and gently lifted her daughter out of what must have been bad dreams, saying don't cry Baby Girl, Mama's here.

Delie took an old ragged quilt Delie's Grandmama Rebekah Sarah had pieced together years before Delie was born, wrapped it around them both and went out to the old porch swing. The evening had been warm but the night had turned crisp, though not the biting cold of the night before—there would be no ice in the well bucket in the morning.

The swinging and Delie's songs lulled Baby Girl into a calm sleep. Even though Delie's bare feet felt the chill of the night air, she kept reaching down to touch the porch floor, moving the swing as gentle as a rocker. Sat there thinking of a name for her daughter besides Baby Girl. But no names came.

She knew she should go in and try to sleep. She knew she had a long day of work ahead of her at Doc Walker's house. And she could feel the deepness of Baby Girl's sleep, deep enough to get her through the night. Still, Delie sat there swinging, sat there in the dark swinging, sat there singing songs to this sleeping daughter with no name, songs very old women had sung to her very old grandmothers when they themselves were very young girls.

Sat there swinging and wishing she had been privileged to see Samuel Daniel, her brother-in-law, look that white man in the eye, look that white man straight on with eyes dark as muscadines, look at him in front of God and everybody, wishing she had seen him reach out and touch that ball, seen him send it hurling into the heavens. Sat there wishing those things, and more, as she sang those very old songs, songs that drifted across Bethel—which the whites called Chickenham—before lifting, rising to the ridge, floating over the soft-lit houses of Sugars Spring, invisible, silent, heavy. Like the scent of jasmine. Or magnolia.

The colored women, some young, and some whose gait told their age, made their nightly journey down the slanted rose-colored road in the pink and blue sunset, the journey from Sugars Spring proper where they spent the days scrubbing floors and weeding gardens and washing and starching and hanging clothes on clotheslines or bushes or wooden fences and ironing clothes and cooking meals and beating rugs strung over clotheslines. They walked past Cora Emery, returning her nod or uplifted hand, and some exchanged words with her about how hot it had been or what the sky foretold for weather tomorrow.

They walked past Cora Emery's to the bottom-land that was Bethel, where the very old women having pulled weeds out of their own gardens and maybe shelled a mess of peas for supper and then sat on porches watching the very young children skittering about the yard, sat waiting for their grand-daughters or daughters to come walking down the road from Sugars Spring. Or they waited for men to come home from the timber, or they waited for men and women and older children to come home from the few fields that were not yet planted.

After cooking and serving supper to the men and then taking their own, after dishes and sweeping and mopping, the very old women and their daughters or granddaughters sat out on the porch, mending and darning and watching the very young play kick the can in the yards or chasing the lightning bugs flickering across the fields. They sat watching the west, through the scatter of trees, turn from pink to the color of the wild red roses that fenced Safronia Grant's yard.

And watched the young men, ripe with youth,

oil their hair and their horses to a shine and set off down the dirt road, their horses prancing like they were in a parade as they passed by the three churches and the one store in Bethel, passed by on their way to Blue Heaven. They watched some of the young women slather flower water on themselves and flounce down that same road, past the Church of Christ, the AME Church, the Bethel Baptist Tabernacle Church and Lincoln Bradley's store, their hair glossed and gleaming.

And the women watched the very old men left to linger under the horse-apple tree, filing handsaws, or bucksaws, or mending mule harnesses, or throwing horseshoes, or packing tobacco in their pipes. The women watched the old men do these things and watched the old men watching the young ones polished up shinier than their horses.

The very old women told the younger women what they'd seen. The old women said if Sammy Dan didn't start taking stock of his actions he'd bring trouble down on their heads as surely as God was up in Heaven's abode. They said he's a married man with children of his own. They said he finally got baptized, just last year. They said in spite of all that, Samuel Daniel seemed to feel beholden, from time to time—like the baseball game—to look trouble in the face, to tempt the devil.

And one old woman with hair that looked like cotton bolls said he better keep any of his wanderings—*if* he be the wandering kind—to his own kind or he'll get strung up for sure.

One of the younger women said what you mean *if,* don't try to tell me he ain't messed around, ain't no man that don't mess around.

They'se some, the old woman with cotton hair said.

Name one, the young woman who had just kicked her husband out of the house said. Safronia Grant, a very old woman, giggling in anticipation of what she was going to say, put two fingers in front of her mouth and said law me, I would mess around too. Course I mean if I was young again.

An old woman with a crooked finger and a green bandana said even if he don't go round with women, he still gotta learn some things if he plan to live to tell stories to his grandkids, why he done gone and got hisself shot once down in Louisiana for not moving his wagon out of a white man's way.

The others agreed. And as the tiredness settled into their bones, they watched the sun go down, watched as the sunset behind the trees of the swamp, which had been the color of Safronia Grant's roses, darkened to the color of vetch, then expanded and sprawled across the western horizon like thistledown, before sliding off the sky. And soon the moon hung there like a giant lantern.

They said he was the spittin' image of his great-uncle, Ransom, who had caused the awful riot nearly forty years ago getting a slew of their own— and only one white man—killed. They said in all their born days they'd never seen nothin' quite like it. They said lawdy, he sure did hit that ball far.

2

Red Sky at Morning

*And in the morning, it will be foul weather
today: for the sky is red and lowring.*

Matthew 16:3

APRIL 2, 1920

Years after, everyone that still had living memory of the storm of April 2, 1920, always talked about the strangeness of a red sky at morning following on the tail of a red sky at night. Safronia Grant, who had watched nightfall come from her porch in Chickenham, professed to be the one who remarked that a red sky at morning was in direct confrontation to the promises of the Bible since the sky the night before had looked ablaze, looked like a raging fire. She said we ain't had a sky so red since a year ago to this exact day. Safronia knew it was a year ago to the day because the fiery sunset had occurred the day of the baseball game which was also

31

the day of the twenty-fifth wedding anniversary of her oldest granddaughter. After the storm Safronia professed often to have said that to the other women as they gathered together to go clean the church.

But several of the others wiping the benches or even the younger ones who could get on their knees to oil laid claim to having said part or all of Safronia's statement themselves.

And everybody in Sugars Spring old enough to remember always said the sky that morning turned as red as Isannah Sanders' hair. Lottie Ellis, Cora Emery McRae's nearest white neighbor in the valley, even laid claim to making that exact remark when she looked out her kitchen window after breakfast, said she told Milton I declare the sun stuck its head up earlier but changed its mind and now it's as red as Isannah Sanders' hair. But Milton never said yes indeed she did when she turned to him and said didn't I say those exact words Milton. He'd just say it was something like that.

That's how Lottie Ellis always saw it, as a case of the sun having a simple change of mind after having begun the day as gentle as one of her husband's prayers. By the time Ham, her black rooster, woke her and probably most of the valley, the sun had washed out the black night and left the sky a soft gray. And by the time she emerged from the barn, the sky had turned as white as a lemon-bleached sheet, and her tin bucket, heavy with Ol' Jersey's milk, caught specks of sun and sent them scattering in the clear morning air.

For the next hour Lottie was occupied with helping Milton with his toilet. She rubbed him down with boiled grapevine water suggested by Crazy Sadie—the blackest woman in Chickenham, black as her African daddy—to soothe the misery in his back. She helped him use the night pan, she dressed him, walked him to the kitchen, set him down at their round pine table and—after he said grace, thanking God for another day with his loved one—served them both up a bowl of hot oatmeal laden with butter and cream and sugar syrup.

Milton ate three helpings and Lottie marveled at how becalmed his spirit was despite bein' gnarled up like a cypress knee and in pain every waking moment of his life. She was praying the warm spring weather and milkweed tea would loosen his joints and allow him to get about some, or at least provide some pleasant days for him to while away on the front porch.

It was when she took their empty bowls to the dry sink that she noticed the haze, pink as a tea rose, between their house and the barn. She said that is mighty strange and her husband said what, and she said that the sky had gotten red all of a sudden. A red morning following the coattail of a red night sure is strange she said. Besides, she said, the sun was out as big as you please an hour ago—guess it must have changed its mind. Then Milton smiled and said well he guessed maybe that was the sun's prerogative. And she smiled at that and poured the milk from the bucket into the butter churn.

On the way to the wellhouse with a plate of freshly churned butter and a small milk can of buttermilk she noticed the red was gone, the sky was yellow green, the color of a dying plant, and the clouds in the southwest—just above the trees that shaded the Chickenham shacks—looked dark and deep like evil incarnate.

Lottie stood there, between the wellhouse and her back porch, looking like a rabbit who just hopped into a meadow and finds itself caught between a huntin' dog in one direction and the hunter in the other, stood there not knowing whether to proceed to the wellhouse with the freshly churned butter and buttermilk, or go back inside to try to lead her crippled husband to their storm cellar.

Montgomery Sugars had been up for hours, hauling her two grown daughters, the war-widowed one with lavender eyes and the unmarried one with ivory skin, out of bed even before their banty rooster climbed up on his perch on the fence railing to yell at the sun as it rose over the red bank to shed soft light on their farm. Gol durn, you split-tails, she said as she yanked the quilt off her daughters' bed causing them to curl up like roley-poleys, wake me and your daddy both up in the dead of night with

your babel after gallivantin' from here to kingdom
come. Get outa that bed right now and put on your
barn boots. Y'all're gonna wish you'd let me get a
good night's sleep before this day is over.

They knew better than to argue or to suggest
that it would not hurt their baby brother, David
Ben, home intact from the war and healthy as their
young bull, Buck, to help—having long since
learned that their mother, a tiny sun-wrinkled
woman who dressed in starched unbleached cotton
dresses and oversized boots, would brook anything
from her girls except whining and laziness and com-
plaints against the menfolks. So the grown daughters, the first girls in town to bob their nutmeg hair
for the sake of fashion instead of from sickness, the
only ones who had abandoned corsets, and would
soon be the first to let the waist of their dresses slide
down to their hips, to let the hems shrink way up
their legs—still rosy-cheeked and red-lipped from
the night before—slid out of their flannel night-
gowns and into their coveralls and followed their
mama out to the barn.

After we get done milkin', we're gonna muck
out and then we got some fence mendin' to do
before we go milk deliverin', Montgomery said as
she plopped down on her blackgum stool in the first
stall, grabbed two teats of her best Jersey with her
tiny rugged hands, brown as an acorn, and tugged
the milk out in a torrent which planked as it hit the
bottom of the pail.

The war-widowed daughter who always doused herself with the scent of magnolia looked at the unmarried one who preferred lilac water, gave a big sigh and rolled her lavender eyes up at the sky that had been orange with the moon just hours before, but now was moonless and colorless except for a ribbon of red in the southwest. It's going to be a long day she said to her sister in a whisper as quiet as a cat's walk.

They were done with milking, and mucking and pounding two cedar fence posts, and were scouring for bitterweed in the pasture that angled down behind their house when Montgomery became suspicious of the blue-black clouds lurking in the southwest and said she reckoned they'd better go get the men up and get in the storm cellar until it blew over. Halfway up the hill, in the elbow of the slope—where the old well stood—still a good hundred yards from the house, the unmarried one with ivory skin looked back across the valley and saw the cloud spin out a mare's tail, saw it dip down low enough to lift the tin roof off the Flowers' barn like it was a sheet of paper. She hollered that it was a cyclone and Montgomery looking back said goddammit and dropped the posthole digger she had slung over her shoulder and yelled run.

The daughters didn't look back until they reached the storm cellar, which was about thirty yards from the house—next to where the old Sugars plantation house had been before lightning burned it to the ground. By then, the cloud was hugging the ground, rolling like an automobile tire toward Cora Emery's tiny white house in the heart of the valley. The daughters pulled the rope anchored with a sand-filled bucket to open the door, descended the steps into the red clay room no bigger than their pantry. They stood in a corner with their arms around each other, mixing the scent of damp earth and lilac and magnolia and cow manure—not saying anything to each other, but knowing they both were praying for their mama who was running, like one of their banty hens being chased by their rooster, toward the house to wake her sleeping men.

Cora Emery McRae had sat on her front porch steps the night before, had watched the sky turn from ivory to a soft yellow, the color of a pear, before turning to pink, then to red in a matter of minutes. She had watched sunsets here for twenty years, but for some reason the red sky seemed to be the exact color of the berry of the wintergreens she hadn't seen in twenty years, for some reason those few minutes of pink sky reminded her of the tourmaline ring she had as a child but couldn't for the life of her remember what had happened to it, or even if she'd brought it with her when she came as a young lady to a place where land, and sky, could change from white to red to black, could change as sudden as life changed to death.

She heard the tinging sound of horseshoes and

she thought for an instant that the sound was the sound of her grandfather tossing horseshoes up into the Maine sky. The sound was so strong in her memory that it took awhile for her to realize that it came from Bethel.

The sound might as well, though, have been coming from Maine for all the longing it triggered in Cora Emery. Over the years, she had often thought of herself as an ocean salmon trapped behind a creek dam on its way back to sea. She had even told her husband that once, and he had laughed the easy, rippling laugh that made her love him all the more. Even though laughing out loud just wasn't in her blood, just like Sugars Spring wasn't in her blood and never would be.

Still, here she was, twenty years after coming to this the land of the many-colored soils—the clay of the ridge that overlooked her house and other houses in the valley, the clay that with the slant of the sun changed from soft brown to golden pink, to rose red, to magenta. And the rich bottomland soil that yielded grass, tall and luminous. Black soil it was, blacker than night, blacker than sin, her friend Rebekah Sarah had once said. Gray soil too, the color of slate. And soil white as chalk in the flatland that those who came there called the prairie, white as bride's breath.

Here she was, having thought she was going to be here for just one day, here she was sitting on her porch steps, situated where the many colors of land

and road collided with one another, situated between Bethel and Sugars Spring, really one township, but two distinct communities, separated by
custom and by law and by choice, separated by the
color of their skin, even by the color of the soil, by
both enmity and politeness, separated even in their
churches, and by so many other lines. But twined
too, in ways she would never fully understand,
twined by the same strings that marked the lines of
separation, strings as visible and strong as rope,
strings invisible, almost, like fine silk thread, or the
gossamer of a spider's web. Twined by blood even.

She had sat, the night before as on many other
nights, on her steps and looked at the land and
watched the sunset and breathed in the scent of jasmine drifting through the air in the last light of day
and listened to the faint sounds of singing and the
tinging of horseshoes floating over the pasture between her house and Chickenham, breathed in the
smell of boiling maple sap wafting through the
spring seasons of her New England childhood and
remembered the sound of melting ice washing
against the granite rocks on the shore of Crystal
Lake in Harrison, Maine, where her aunt and uncle
had lived, a tinkling sound, like tiny Christmas
bells.

And being assured—because the night sky was
now as red as the river, indeed as red as Isannah
Sanders' hair—that the morrow would be a fair
day, Cora Emery had risen early that morning of

April sixth and walked the bottom road to Chickenham to ask Rebekah Sarah, the old, old colored
woman with one eye green and one eye brown if she
would come help out with spring cleaning which
both women knew meant that they would, more
than anything else, give company to each other the
way they had on occasion since Rebekah Sarah had,
as she put it, been put out to pasture like an ol' mule
when she was replaced by her daughter and then a
granddaughter as the cleaning woman and cook for
old Doc Walker's family.

Cora Emery and Rebekah Sarah had walked
down a back road, a pasture trail really, comment-
ing on the profusion of chiggerweed by the edge of
the path, Cora Emery reminding herself that twenty
years ago she had known them only as black-eyed
susans, and were ambling down the cow path in
Clinton Flowers' pasture toward Cora Emery's
when Rebekah Sarah stopped. She closed her
brown eye, scanned the sky with her green eye the
color of swamp water and said somethin' ain't
right.

Cora Emery seeing the cloud hiding behind the
cypress trees near Mossy Lake, a cloud as violet as
the fields of vetch along the roadsides of Buckfield,
Maine, sucked in her breath but only said I believe
it's going to rain after all today, Rebekah Sarah,
maybe we best wait another day to beat the rugs,
come I'll walk you back home.

Ain't no need, Rebekah Sarah said. But of

course I will, Cora Emery said, taking Rebekah Sarah's arm as wrinkled and as soft as worn leather and turning her gently toward her home.

Ain't no need for you to walk me, Rebekah Sarah said again, that cloud got evil in it but it ain't gonna bother my person this time.

Cora Emery, who didn't force words on people, and was noted for being untalkative herself—which had caused a considerable resentment when she first came to Sugars Spring, but which twenty years later was accepted as a Yankee oddity to be pitied—kept on walking beside Rebekah Sarah, kept on walking as she listened, again, to Rebekah Sarah's story that today seemed to pour from her like rain from a heavy-laden cloud.

Rebekah Sarah had been seeing things since she was a tiny slave child, mostly bad things like storms and sickness, floods and death. The first time it happened she told her mama about it, saying Mama, Papa's gonna die and the whole world's gonna be black with grief. And her mama had said go on wicha chile, don't be saying such forebodin' things. Now hush yore mouth. But Rebekah Sarah wouldn't hush her mouth no matter how many times her mama told her to. Then her mama looked Rebekah Sarah in the eye and said I done tol' you to hush girl, and she squeezed Rebekah Sarah's small shoulders and shook her body hard enough to lift her feet clear off the ground. And when Rebekah Sarah still wouldn't cease her tongue even though her mama had shaken her, her mama gave her one hard swat across her bottom sayin' better one lick from yore mama than bein' tied to a tree and horse-whipped by a master one of these days.

That very afternoon, the sky turned the color of blackbirds and stars tumbled out of it. The cows, thinking it was nightfall, came home in the middle of the day and the chickens went to roost. Rebekah Sarah could still look back in her memory and see people running around screaming oh lawd the day of judgment done come upon us. She could look back and see one old, old woman, too old to go to the fields, sitting on a porch laughing and shouting hallelujah Jesus comin' at last.

Rebekah Sarah told Cora Emery she still re-membered her mama fretting and pacing about the master's house shining the black cherry furniture but all the time fearing the truth of her daughter's prophecy. And as soon as the master took his family to church to pray, her mama ran like a rabbit to-ward the big field searching for her man. When she got to the end of the lane out of breath from running and from fear of the death the darkness was an-nouncing, there Rebekah Sarah's daddy was, driv-ing a wagon, coming from a fetching errand in town, as alive and healthy as you please and not the least bit 'feared of the day darkness.

Rebekah Sarah could still look back and see her daddy jumping down from the wagon. She could still see her mama reaching the wagon where the bean tree shaded the lane and as soon as her daddy hopped down her mama locked her arms about his neck tight as a snapping turtle until she remembered Rebekah Sarah who was standing in the lane looking at her daddy, trying with all her might to keep her eyes closed to block out the vision of her daddy's body that still floated across the green one.

Rebekah Sarah's mama came running at her, grabbed her by her shoulders and shook her, screaming don'tcha ever, ever scare the livin' daylights outa me again.

Rebekah Sarah had never told any white person and not many of her own people about her green eye until Cora Emery started calling on her for help when Rebekah Sarah was put aside by Doc Walker's family. And even though she'd told Cora Emery the story of her daddy's death several times before, Cora Emery listened—out of politeness—as if she were hearing it for the first time. Besides it helped Cora keep her mind off the day darkness that seemed to be descending on them as well.

First Mama slap me for the second time that day—Rebekah Sarah said as if she were telling of a wrong done just the day before—and then she likta pull me bald-headed but I didn' wail one bit even though I can still hear the sound of that whack sometime if I lets myself think back. And sometime my head get so sore I don' know why. But then I remember and then I know. But I shore didn' shed not one tear—jus' stood looking at Mama *hard* the way preachers look at you when they stop in the middle of their yellin', stop and let it be so quiet you can hear a mosquito flying, to make sure you got time enough to feel all full of sin. Then my daddy pull her off me and say why she go and slap me so unprovoked, but Mama jus' look over at me and say she know why. And Mama be thinkin' that's that.

But it ain't. That night while we sleepin' men come ridin' up on horses. In my sleep it be thunder, and they holler nigger come out here and Mama say to Daddy run out the back door but Daddy say ain't no place to run to and he walk out on the porch to face the horde of men what come after him jus' like a pack of huntin' dogs. And Mama run like a streak of lightnin' to the big house to beg the master for help but it didn' taken my green eye to know no matter how hard my daddy worked his whole life, no matter that Daddy was the most valuable slave he have, the master wadn' gonna stop those men, that he wadn' even gonna try.

And sure nuf he say to Mama he cain't do nothin', he say they be a limit to what he can do for her.

And Daddy died not knowing exactly what thing he be accused of even though he knew the general nature by all the name callin' they be doin' as they hang him. We come to know about the judge's wife later. She walked by just as Daddy come out the store to load the seed on the wagon, and she claim he gave her an insinuatin' look, so insinuatin' it chill her bones, so insinuatin' it'd take many a night before she could sleep again. So they hang my daddy from the horsechestnut tree in front of the courthouse—but not before they cut off his manlihood. In my dream it be a wildcat screamin' down in the swamp—my daddy was a big man, but in my dream he sound like a little ol' wildcat out prowlin' on a black night.

Cora Emery, her hand still on Rebekah Sarah's elbow, tried not to notice the cloud had moved from south to west, tried not to notice the ragged edges as green as Rebekah Sarah's eye, tried to keep her mind on the story falling from Rebekah Sarah like heavy rain.

Mama wadn' never herself t'all after and she be all the time thinkin' because I let those words cross my lips that death come to Daddy. She say my eye be drivin' her mind away, be drivin' her to the devil and she axe the master to sell me and he do. As a favor to her. And because I look him in the eye one day, saw straight to where his soul oughta be—and he knowed it. And the ones what bought me taken me on a wagon and then on a rowboat and then on a boat as big as Noah's to New Or-leens, a boat that musta been as big as the one what taken my daddy from Africa when he wadn' no more than a boy himself. Then they taken me up the river on a river-boat and sold me on a stump in Fulton. That stump might still be there. And here I been all these years.

Cora Emery wanted to say something to Rebekah Sarah, but she didn't know whether to console an old woman wandering around in the storm of her past, or to try to allay the fear Rebekah Sarah surely must feel as the cloud behind them covered any remnants of sunshine, causing the sky to turn dark. Not as dark as the day Rebekah Sarah spoke of, which must have been the eclipse that Cora Emery's grandparents had witnessed, but dark as the banks of Yellow Creek. Instead of offering words, Cora Emery squeezed Rebekah Sarah's arm to let her know she was still listening.

I never seen my mama or any of my own again. 'Cept with this eye. I seen when she pass and I seen when my brothers and sisters pass, all of them pass on years since. I seen when that train gonna kill yore man, but they was no need to tell you. And I seen yore son dead in the war, dead in a deep ditch in a faraway place before that letter come to you, but I most never tell what I sees with my green eye. But I can tell you this, my granddaughter Delie and her kids gonna get carried away by this wind. And we ain't. And it's gonna take my house and yore house. And Miz Isannah, she gonna whirl through the sky, whirl through the sky just like one of those red dust storms from Texas. And there ain't nothin' for us to do about it. The hoodoo doctor, he cain't do nothin' bout those things. Crazy Sadie cain't neither. Even if I plucks out this eye, my Delie still gonna be dead. They ain't nothin' none of us can do bout what gonna happen. 'Cept grieve. I still gots plenty of grievin' head of me.

For some reason, Cora Emery believed Rebekah Sarah's prophecy—even though Rebekah Sarah had the scent of blackberry brandy on her breath this early in the morning, even though Rebekah Sarah sometimes claimed her daddy was a white man, the master to be exact, and gave her that green eye, even though Rebekah Sarah sometimes said her mama was prostrate with grief when they sold her away, even though Cora Emery's son had died in Cora Emery's arms, coughing his little life right out of him when he was five years old, even though Cora Emery's husband had fallen dead at their well—so she didn't try to dissuade Rebekah Sarah. Instead, she kept her hand on the old woman's elbow and the two women walked at a turtle's pace down the cow path lined with chigger-weed as yellow as egg yolks—walked away from Cora Emery's house where the cyclone was heading, and toward Rebekah Sarah's house where the cloud had passed over.

The cloud had already passed over Samuel Daniel McElroy's tent before Montgomery Sugars and her daughters saw it, before it was in sight of Cora Emery McRae and Rebekah Sarah, who was the grandmother to his wife Estherlee.

Since he lived several miles to the south in Hayden's Landing, he sometimes stayed the night at the work site in the thick woods near Mossy Lake, the swamp that was the backdrop to Bethel, that backed up, in fact, into the backyard of his mother-in-law's house, and into the backyard of Delie, his wife's sister. His wife Estherlee and his four children, and his mother-in-law Phoenicia, had left two days before to attend a weekend reunion of Phoenicia's departed husband's relatives in Ozan. He would not have been there to watch the cloud pass overhead had he not decided to escape the restlessness of the empty house by seeking refuge in a worn canvas tent standing next to the makeshift mule shed. He had slept fully clothed to allow for the lack of blankets, and the warmth of Estherlee's body. Or anyone else's.

Still, he wasn't clothed enough to sleep through the sharpest chill of the night which came, as always, just before dawn causing him to shiver and causing his mind to wander to places it shouldn't be, so he arose and built a fire. By the time the others arrived at daylight, he had the mules harnessed and ready to begin another day.

As the foreman, he had set the others to work and was checking the neck of the team of young mules he himself was breaking in when the shafts of light cutting through the trees began to disappear— one by one at first and then falling away like a stack of dominoes causing it to turn so dark, the thought darted across Samuel Daniel's mind that it might be night coming in the day like the one his Grandmama Mahala McElroy had spoken of when she was very old and he was very young. Indeed, he thought of her as he turned his face straight up, turned to look up to the top and beyond the tall trees, beyond the overcup oaks, the willows, the cedars reaching out of the earth, the cypress and tupelos, reaching out of moss the color of one of his grandmother-in-law's eyes, all of the trees reaching for the hazy yellow sun, reaching into gray and black sky. He thought of his Big Mama Mahala as he looked past the trees into sky, thought of her hair heavy and black and gray swirling around her head like a storm cloud as she sat on the porch telling her stories, thought of her hair swirling around his head as she whispered a name in his ear one night while he slept, whispered a name years before it was his time to know it, whispered a name that was *his* name thinking he was asleep, or knowing he was not, knowing, he suspected, she wouldn't live until his twelfth birthday.

Still, even though he knows she died before then, he remembers her whispering it again at the proper time—on his twelfth birthday—while Great Aunt Crazy Sadie McElroy banged a tin dipper against the pots and pans to keep the spirits from hearing, even though he knows it was his Great-aunt Crazy Sadie whispering and his mother doing the banging. He thought of his Big Mama Mahala

as the cloud rolled ponderously across the top of the
trees before releasing the rain, a heavy rain that
worked its way through the trees, plastering his
broadcloth shirt against his lean body, drenching
him as wet as when he was baptized in Muddy
Creek a little over a year ago, was baptized because
Estherlee had prayed for his salvation, and because
maybe he believed in Jesus part of the time, and because maybe it would wash away the memory of the
night with Delie, Estherlee's sister, would wash
away the sin, would wash away the aching that
never left him even though he loved Estherlee with
all his might. Maybe the baptism had worked in
some small way. At least he had held true to his
promise when he was drenching wet from being
baptized in the waters of Muddy Creek, baptized
into the Bethel Baptist Tabernacle Church, baptized
into the sanctuary offered by Jesus himself, at least
he had held true to his promise to stay away from
Delie's bed, except in a nightmare or a dream he
had a year ago which had been more real than the
time he had known her in the flesh. And that had
occurred *after* he was baptized, so he still had a sin,
a sin of scarlet like they talk about in the Bible, as
scarlet, or as dark as a thunderhead to repent of.
Someday.

Samuel Daniel McElroy shook his head to get
his mind on the job at hand. He shook his head at
the things a storm could conjure up. Then he patted
the young mules on the behind and said it's time
you learned mule talk. He pulled gently but firmly

to the right and said gee. Then he pulled to the left and said haw.

The sun edged through the gaps in the curtains, curtains as dark as loblolly needles, waking Isannah Sanders, who had slept blissfully free of the dread that covered her like a fog and then settled, like lead, in her bones every night when she lay down in bed, lay down beside her husband and began her fall into sleep, marveling that in falling into what should be darkness, the fog actually lifted, the weight of dread became feather light, as she fell, spinning into the dreams of her choosing, spinning her back home in South Carolina, and soon she is riding her horse, black as ebony, down the road shaded by live oaks before bursting into the clearing as the road turns west to the Nathan place and the live oaks disappear leaving her surrounded by fields rich with cotton blossom, her long hair flying behind her like a horse's mane, spinning at a dance as her daddy plays his banjo and taps his foot, as the shy boys with clumsy feet and callused hands, the dapper men in soft suits and twirled moustaches, and even the fat whiskered married men with wives tired out and fanning ask her to dance and she says I'd be delighted, and she dances with them all, reel after reel, and never tires.

She got lighter with each song, lighter as her feet lifted off the floor, lighter still as she floated on a cotton cloud, floated until Baby William woke her demanding to be fed. She smelled the wood smoke grown stale on her husband's night clothes. The sour breath from old snuff. Then the fog started to slither into the room, so she slipped out of bed before it could cover her again.

After she gave William a tin cup of milk and a cold biscuit to hold him, she built a fire in the kitchen stove, heated water, poured it into a white enameled bowl and took it and a bottle of rose water with her to the outhouse to wash herself free of her husband. She had long ago washed away most memory of when he was a handsome widower paying court to her, when she mistook a flame in his eye for love, when she mistook persistence for devotion, when she mistook silence for gentleness.

She had tried to refuse him once, pleading a need for sleep, but he turned her body onto its back and smothered her with his body and the more she tried to push him away, the heavier he became, smothering her body, telling her to stop her writhing, telling her to lay still, all the time quoting scripture in her ear, telling her to remember the book of Ephesians says *wives, submit yourselves unto your own husbands, as unto the Lord,* quoting scripture even as she ceased her writhing and remained perfectly still, stroking her red hair and saying softly, the way he sometimes lowered his voice at the end of a sermon pleading for the lost souls in the congregation to remember Jesus loved those who came to him with repentance in their hearts, saying in a voice as soft as his smooth dry hands that, like the Bible says, she was the weaker vessel, reminding her sweetly as he stroked her hair the Apostle Paul had said *wives be in subjection to your own husbands in all things.* The pain as he entered her was even more searing than on their wedding night. And there was no way to measure the shame.

But at least she had William. William with hair as shiny as a gold coin, William who giggled when she tossed him into the air, William who put his chubby hand into her mouth and pulled her hair as long as Rapunzel's and red as an apple, William who squeezed her breasts with his tiny hands. At least her husband—old enough to be her father—had given her William. And he'd no doubt give her more.

Her husband sat at his desk preparing Sunday's sermon—about Eve and the serpent—while she fixed hotcakes, and heated sorghum, and fried thick slabs of bacon, and for some reason she could never name she decided that this morning she would not pin up her hair, redder than the river, before she called him to breakfast—even though she knew it would anger him that she had left her hair long and flowing and that she was still in her chemise nightgown, white and soft as down, even though she knew when evening came, when he chose the Bible reading, he would choose the scripture that said a woman should not use her hair for adornment, and he would remind her how his sister with hair, too, as red as brimstone had brought shame to him back in South Carolina with her two bastard children, how his father had disgraced them all by taking his sister—and her children—under his roof, and how he would see his own wife dead and in the ground before he saw her become like his sister.

Later in the lightless bedroom, curtained with heavy green to keep out the moon which hung over this land he'd brought her to with particular brightness, he would reach for her with smooth dry hands and he would cover her like fog and weigh her down like lead and she'd close her mind and pretend she was his sister only he doesn't know it in the darkness of the room and she'd feel evil and dirty but she would still pretend it just the same.

Her husband ate his hotcakes drowned in warmed sorghum and he ate his thick slabs of bacon. Then he said it seemed to him she might fix him some eggs. She said she was sorry but he had said just yesterday he was tired of them. She fried him three eggs with crusty edges the way he liked them while William pulled his hotcakes apart and stuffed them in his mouth and slammed them against the high chair and his father said keep that child quiet.

Then Isannah put the three fried eggs on a clean spatter-blue plate and set it in front of her husband. She took the dirty plates to the dry sink, scraped the bits of hotcake that William had missed getting into his mouth and a tag end of her piece of bacon onto a battered tin plate and stepped out on the back porch to give it to their coon dog, stepped out into air that was green, green like summer light bouncing off the swamp.

She shot her gray eyes to the southwest and saw the cloud, dark as indigo. She dropped the tin plate, and the hotcakes soaked in sorghum scattered on the porch, a piece of hotcake sticking to the top of her bare foot. She rushed into the kitchen and said it's coming up a cloud, said they'd better head for the Huffs' stormhouse and he said not until he'd finished his breakfast and she said please, she said I'm scared, and he said hold quiet woman and let me eat in peace. Then she knew what she had to do. She grabbed William out of his high chair with such a force it turned the high chair over on its side. His tin cup skittered, splattering milk across the length of the kitchen floor like pearls.

She didn't bother with a duster, didn't even think about it. She didn't bother with shoes even though she had a good hundred yards to run, some of it through cuckleburrs. She said then I'm going without you and he said you'll do no such thing, he said simmer down wife, he said he'd go as soon as he had his breakfast but she grabbed William and turned over the high chair and spilled the tin cup that threw splats of milk across the kitchen floor and ran out the door and up the gentle slope of their land toward the Huffs' stormhouse.

*   *   *

The cyclone, black and green and spiteful, seemed to have been born out of the cypress swamp, seemed to have come to life behind Chickenham, seemed to have literally churned itself to life in the green waters. It didn't touch the town of White Bluff on the other side of the swamp—all they had of weather was a dim sky and a few splats of rain before the sun and a warm spring wind nudged the cloud out of sight.

Only a few of the folks in White Bluff or Hayden's Landing even heard the far off thunder of the lightning storm that was dragged along on the tail of the cyclone, so they didn't know a solitary thing about it until the mail carrier came through in his Model T about midmorning and told them of the havoc and devastation that had visited Sugars Spring. They hooked up their wagons, or cranked up their automobiles, or saddled up their horses, and swarmed into Sugars Spring to see who was killed and who was maimed and they prayed please not to let it be anyone they were related to or loved, and the mail carrier continued on his route to deliver the mail and the news to Yellow Creek.

Delie Turner, Rebekah Sarah's youngest granddaughter and the comeliest one too, the one with pecan-colored skin and long hair so black it shone like a blackbird's wings, was the first to be devoured by the cyclone.

She and William Burl Cane—the white man who slept with her—and her boys had eaten left-over squirrel stew for breakfast and William Burl told the boys when they got big enough he would learn them to shoot, learn them to shoot so good they wouldn't even have to hit a squirrel to kill him, they could just bark them, could just hit the limb beneath their feet killing them with the vibrations. He asked what they thought about that. They just nodded their heads up and down and Delie wondered what had possessed William Burl. After they were done eating, William Burl left in his truck to drive to White Bluff for some engine parts, but not before promising to return that evening with a treat of brown sugar candy for them. He said best keep an eye on that cloud as he climbed into his truck. Delie held Baby Girl in her arms and her sons hugged tight to her faded cotton dress as they all waved good-bye to William Burl.

Then Delie felt a chill that had nothing to do with the weather, a blast of cold like a winter storm even though the day was already warm. But she did not yet have the wisdom or power to understand, so she said come on, sweet things, let's go inside.

William Burl could hardly have been out of sight when the cloud, choosing them as its first victims, came down on them, sucking the shack—with them in it—into the sky. Hoss Richards' search party found Delie looking just like she was asleep—and not a mark on her—resting against a sweetgum hundreds of yards on the north side of Mossy Lake which meant that the storm, which for reasons known only to God had spared Chickenham proper, had whirled Delie and her sons and her daughter and her shack up over the town, over Mossy Lake, and deposited them on the other side near Hayden's Landing.

They never did find the remains of one of the sons and assumed the swamp had sucked him deep within its bowels. Young Dr. Harper, who came over from Yellow Creek to help, conjectured that Delie was probably alive until she broke her neck when she came to rest against the sweetgum tree and her sons landed here and yon. He conjectured that she—and maybe her sons—had been able to look down on the cluster of houses in Chickenham proper as if they were mallard ducks flying north for the summer.

They didn't find Baby Girl until evening even though Samuel Daniel McElroy had searched for her, frantically, for hours before leaving to go fetch his wife and his mother-in-law Phoenicia who were at a homecoming in Ozan—and to deliver the bad news.

Shortly before sunset, some colored folks found Baby Girl toddling in the patch of wild roses that surrounded Safronia Grant's house, and which was just a stone's throw from where Delie's house used to be. She had blisters on her feet like she had walked for miles, even though she was barely over two years old, but nobody dared believe she had made the long trip through the sky with her mother and her brothers and somehow found her way home, or almost home—like dogs sometimes do when you give them to someone a long way off.

By some unfathomable miracle, except for the feet, she had only a few scratches, which probably came from toddling about amidst Safronia's wild roses.

William Burl Cane, who came from a good family, who had a mind as sharp as a razor, and who could have had his pick of any number of pretty and even decent white women but seemed bent on turning out sorry, heard the news while he was tuning up David Ben's A Model and dropped his spark plug wrench on the ground, fell to his knees and cried and cried and cried.

Except for swatting Rebekah Sarah's house, the storm ignored the rest of Bethel, which the whites called Chickenham, choosing instead to visit the Flowers place next, but taking only the pitched roof of the barn while the Flowers children stood in the middle of the road—with slates and lunch buckets—and watched. The horses and what was left of the hay in the barn got drenched in the downpour that followed and Clinton Flowers, already forty-two years old and the father of seven living kids, had to put a new roof on the barn, using the money he had saved—coin by coin—for years so that he could study to become a doctor.

The storm moved directly over the Flowers children who watched in awe as their roof flew over them like some great silver-winged bird, who watched in awe as the edge of the ink-black column picked up America Jamison skipping to school in her new yellow gingham dress about a hundred feet ahead of them, picked her up and lifted her, everybody said, at least thirty fect high in the air, and then dropped her a hundred yards from where it had lifted her in the first place. Except Little Jewel Flowers, who at twelve was already known for being levelheaded, maintained it lifted America ten feet and dropped her thirty yards at the most.

America was unhurt except for two skint knees and a long scratch on her stomach that left blood on her yellow gingham dress, blood that wouldn't budge no matter what concoction Miz Jamison used. Thirty-four years later the doctors thought America had cancer until they operated and found a splinter in her intestine that had been there since her ride in the tornado.

Then the storm turned its full wrath toward Cora Emery McRae's place not knowing Cora Emery was safe to the south—walking an old colored woman to her misery. It lifted her small fresh-painted red barn and scattered it in a million pieces throughout the valley. It stole her small white house and pulled her crepe myrtle bush out by the roots and when Cora Emery got there the only sign that a house had been there was her front porch steps, pine steps splintered and faded to gray, that hadn't scooted even an inch—steps leading to a patch of bare dirt, brown as a tow sack and dotted with puddles, a patch of dirt and puddles surrounded by drenched and dirty irises.

Cora Emery sat down on the steps and let out all the air in her lungs. She thought maybe she simply wouldn't bother to take any more air in. Then she thought maybe she would finally go back to New England the way she had threatened to when she and James had come up against the trials of marriage—when their cotton crop failed, when she felt smothered by the steaming heat, when the cockroaches invaded her kitchen no matter how often she scrubbed it with lye soap, when chiggers attacked her as she picked blackberries and left her red and swollen and scratching night after night, when she didn't understand this land that had found new ways to wage a war the history books told her ended years before. And when James looked at young Isannah Sanders, Isannah of the china skin and hair so red not even poets much less Cora Emery could ever describe. She could, though, describe James's look as she had seen it often on her father's face as he sat on a granite rock looking over the hills of Maine, knowing on the other side was the sea.

But Cora Emery had never left at any of those

times. And she had buried, first, her five-year-old
son and only weeks later her stillborn daughter—
and much more recently, her husband—buried
them all near the black cherry tree on the northeast
edge of the cemetery. So it was only for a few moments that Cora Emery thought she might go back
home before she realized, house or no house, she
was as much at home as she would ever be again.

Cora Emery McRae got up from the steps leading to where she had come as a young woman almost nineteen years before and surveyed what
James had laughingly called their royal domain.
Her rosebushes, too, had all been yanked out of the
ground. Her azalea bush was ravaged, but it might
be saved. Her irises were bent and dirty. Her jonquils, though, stood in the corner of her yard, bright
and clean as if the day had been one of quiet rain
followed by sunshine. Her backyard sweetgum
didn't look as if it had even felt a breeze. Cora
Emery McRae took one more deep breath, squared
her shoulders and tried to decide whether to go to
Sugars Spring proper to help those who had suffered more than the loss of a house, or to go back
and help Rebekah Sarah, and to check on the other
colored folks in Chickenham. She'd look for her
cow and any chickens that might have survived
later.

Lottie Ellis hurried back to the house, careful
not to drop the butter or spill the milk. She told

Milton they had to get to the storm cellar, and he said go on without me dear, he said it would take me a month to walk that far and I suspect it will all be over by then and she said don't be a fool. And while they were arguing, the storm took their neighbors' houses on each side, taking the lives of Otis and Clara Evans and their newborn daughter, but their three-year-old son didn't get a scratch even though they were sleeping in the same bed.

It took the Bells' house and left their chickens running around without a feather on them and a piece of tin of the Flowers' barn roof pierced as clean as an arrow through their sycamore tree, but the five Bells huddled under their feather bed were all spared.

It took only the Ellis's wellhouse and their catawba tree that shaded the south side of their front porch while they argued in the kitchen, and Lottie always maintained she forever after felt sinful that she paused if only for a second trying to decide whether to go to the wellhouse to store her milk and butter or to the house to be with her husband. Milton said secin' how the storm took the wellhouse he guessed she made the right decision.

Montgomery Sugars ran with the speed of a rabbit to her house. She grabbed the screen door handle and turned for one look, like Lot's wife must have done even though she must have known it would be an awful sight, turned to see the cloud, now past Cora Emery's and coughing out all manner of debris, swerve sharply to the right and head directly at her. She knew, then, she and her men would never have time to make it to the storm cellar, so she didn't see any point in waking them. She kept her hand on the screen door handle as if somehow that would anchor and protect her. She shook her fist at the dark and evil funnel coming toward her and hollered goddammit you'll rue the day you take my house.

As if it heard her, the funnel—black as mud—lifted off the ground, bounced over their house and didn't drop down again until it got to the Cummings who were safe and sound in their storm cellar.

It roared with the sound of a midnight train and whammed into the Methodist church on the edge of Sugars Spring proper destroying the building but leaving most of the benches exactly where they always were on Sunday mornings. Then it sped toward a small gray house in the middle of a sloping field where Isannah Sanders was running—in her thin gown and barefooted, with Baby William in her arms—up the slope. And where her husband was finishing his breakfast.

Isannah Sanders heard the sound of the freight train behind her as she ran toward the Huffs'. She knew the cloud was upon her and that she had no hope of making it but she kept running anyway and soon she didn't hear anything—she didn't hear the train, she didn't hear the thunder that tailed the cloud and shook the valley—it was like she was deaf. Except for a voice—a woman's voice—clear, strong too, yet as soft as satin, saying with all the calm of a star-filled summer night *hold on to your baby, hold on.* Isannah felt the force of the wind at her back and the last thing she remembered was being lifted off the ground, higher and higher. The only thing she saw was a swirl of colors—the white of the houses on the ridge, the green of trees and grass, the red clay ditches, the pink of the dogwood, the hydrangeas purple from the rusty nails hammered near their roots, the yellow field flowers, the coffee-colored cow pond in Ervin Robertson's pasture, even the gray of the house where her husband was finishing his breakfast swirled into a ribbon of colors like adding tints to a bucket of paint and then, even though she was certain her eyes were still open, swirled into total black.

She and William flew through the darkness. She heard the voice one more time say *don't let go of your son* just as something snagged her hair and jerked her abruptly out of the cloud. Then black swirled to white, only white as her gray eyes locked open as wide as a deer's. And the voice didn't speak to her anymore. But no matter, by then Isannah Sanders' fingers were locked to William as firm as any vise at Pleasant Gilbert's store.

*   *   *

Samuel Daniel McElroy, who had joined the
search parties when Cousin Rooster's wife came
running to the woods to see if they were harmed,
and was with the ones who found Delie near where
he lived on the other side of the swamp, on the other
side of Sugars Spring. He picked her up from her
spot beneath the sweetgum tree, picked her up and
carried her, not through the fields and bottomland
but on the trail that led to the red clay road that rose
and arched through Sugars Spring, carried her in his
arms, even though Hoss Richards and others walking beside him said let me carry her part of the way,
carried her in his long arms even though young Doc
Harper said let me put her in the backseat of my
automobile and take her to her mother's, carried
her through the heart of Sugars Spring, not looking
at any of the whites who, caught in the light of the
sun that had followed the rain, were scurrying like
cockroaches trying to find their chickens, or their
children, or trying to find out which was the worst
or best place to go to first, carried her through
Bethel proper, past the Bethel Baptist Tabernacle
Church where he had been baptized, and where
Delie sat every Sunday, sat beside her sister Estherlee—who was his wife—and prayed for forgiveness,
carried her to the home of Phoenicia, who being
gone to Ozan with his wife and kids and not having
the sight of her mother, would not yet know that
she had one less child gracing the earth.

When he walked up the path, Rebekah Sarah was standing in the doorway. He had known, somehow, she would be there waiting for her granddaughter Delie. And waiting for him. He placed Delie on Phoenicia's bed, letting her body roll from his arms onto the patchwork quilt that Delie and his wife and their mama Phoenicia and Phoenicia's mama Rebekah Sarah—who old as she was still had sight enough to stitch—had quilted just the fall before, stitching together pieces of the dresses the women in Sugars Spring handed down with bits of their own go-to-meeting dresses they had made themselves, stitching them all together in patterns handed down and patterns of their own choosing, laid her down on the brightly colored quilt, her hair gleaming like a wet eagle, and spreading like wings about her head.

Samuel Daniel McElroy sat there on the edge of the bed seeing nothing but Delie. Rebekah Sarah sat in the rocker beside the bed, rocking—seeing what only she could see.

Soon they saw other women, old and not so old, coming up the road that turned from red to black between where Rebekah Sarah's house had been and Phoenicia's house. With no word passing between them, Rebekah Sarah stood and began to undress her granddaughter, the prettiest one living or dead, who had the same smooth pecan-colored skin she had once had, began to undress her so that she could wash her just as she had washed so many of the dead.

Samuel Daniel McElroy walked out the door and went down to ask Ernest Stone Junior if he would drive him to Ozan to fetch his wife and his kids and her mother. Taking a wagon would take too long. But then, everything from now on would take too long.

Mr. Davis Huff and David Ben Sugars were the first to spot Isannah Sanders, hanging by her waist-length hair, hair the color of blood, hair the color of yesterday's sunset, in the top of the black oak, the only tree on the slope. The lightning storm that followed the cyclone had already passed and now it was simply raining, so she would had to have been hanging there at least half an hour. Her gray eyes looked glazed, like marble. Her chemise gown was wet and see-through and plastered against her body. William had slipped from the lock of her arms, his tiny arms clasped tightly around her thighs. Her arms were stretched out full length and her hands gripped her son's arms at his shoulders.

They yelled at her not to move, not to stir in case her hair untangled and she dropped thirty feet to the ground. David Ben Sugars in his voice as sweet as sorghum cane said over and over just hang on Miz Isannah—even though they were about the same age—just hang on, we've got a ladder comin' to you. You're gonna be just fine.

It took awhile, but finally they came with the

tallest ladder in town, finally David Ben Sugars ascended the ladder and after more quiet talking convinced Isannah to release her grip on Baby William's arms. But even when she would, she could not. It took all of David Ben's strength to pry her hands loose. He took William and passed him down to someone who passed him down to someone who passed him down to Miz Abigail Huff. Then he put his arm around Isannah's waist and lifted her to draw the weight from her hair but her hair would not untangle from around the branch— so Floyd Dillard climbed the tree, climbed out on the limb and with his Barley knife cut her free.

Strands of red hair were still wrapped around that tree when some children climbed out on a limb of that black oak more than twenty years later.

Little William started to yowl as soon as Miz Abigail Huff took him even though she shielded him from the rain with her silver umbrella, prompting twelve-year-old Little Jewel Flowers to say may I take him Miz Abigail and as soon as Little Jewel took him and put her face against his he stopped crying.

David Ben brought Isannah down like a sack of flour slung over his shoulder, and when he set her down on the ground her drenched gown clung to her like skin and David Ben should have looked away but he didn't.

Then someone put a brown wool blanket around Isannah and she felt comforted even though it was sopping wet. We got to take her inside to get dry someone said. Then they waited in the rain and the quiet for someone to tell her the dreadful news.

From where they all stood, the Sanders house looked completely unscathed, but the storm had taken the kitchen from the back of the house like slicing a piece of cake. The men had found her husband—and the minister to some of them—where the kitchen had been, with a two-by-four pierced through his head, in almost geometric precision, entering the left side and exited the right—or so they surmised by the blood on only the right side.

Finally, in fits and starts—like a pan of oatmeal trying to boil—they managed to tell Isannah the sad and awful truth.

That's when they realized the toll Isannah's ordeal had exacted from her. Isannah didn't respond at first—she just sat there in the rain with the wet brown wool blanket wrapped around her. Sat there looking out into space, looking like there was nothing running around in that beautiful head of hers, looking, they hesitated to say, like she was almost smiling.

Isannah Sanders sat there hearing the words fluttering about but not putting two and two together to understand what they were saying, sat there hearing their words but listening, still, for the voice that had spoken to her, sat there wondering if the colored man called Samuel Daniel McElroy had truly walked through the frozen glaze of her eyes carrying a sleeping Delie Turner who she knew mostly by name, but had heard comforting her baby daughter one day at Pleasant Gilbert's store, sat there wondering why Delie Turner's voice was running together with the voice in the clouds, sat there not daring to wonder why a colored man walked through her gray and frozen and unseeing eyes, a colored man with skin the color of ripe muscadines, sat there not daring to wonder what it was she was feeling when thinking about this same colored man, strong, but lean as a deerhound hitting a baseball clear into Ervin Robertson's persimmon patch, hitting a ball that traveled so far it got caught in the path of the sun and disappeared into the ivory sky before reappearing where the sky was edged with blue and falling like a ripened apple into the persimmon patch. Wondered what she was feeling thinking about a colored man running around the flour-sack bases at the baseball game long ago, sat there remembering her mother's admonishments as to the animal nature of the colored man and how it was her duty as a woman, and a Christian, not to give even the good ones so much as a hint of a smile lest it kindle their lust beyond control, sat there wondering why she felt that same stirring when David Ben Sugars had taken her off his shoulders and placed her on the ground where she now sat huddling underneath a wet wool blanket, sat wondering what in the name of God all the people hovering about her were saying.

Then after about the eighth or ninth time they told her how her kitchen was gone except for the high chair which was standing right in the middle of where the kitchen had been, standing like it hadn' even been blowed over. But other than that, the kitchen was gone and the kitchen porch too—except for the tin plate of dog scraps with the hotcake and bacon scraps still in it, and told her again how her husband had died.

Finally, Isannah Sanders startled, like someone being shook awake from a daytime nap and said what, what's that you say?

When they told her one more time, she looked at her bare feet for a long time. Then she reached down and flicked the piece of hotcake still stuck to the top of her bare foot, broke out into a laugh that could only be called hysterical, took Baby William from Little Jewel Flowers' arms and with the blanket wrapped around them started toward what was left of her house—her laughter pelting the air like sleet.

They all said bless her heart, they all said it was a miracle lightning hadn't struck her when she was hanging there like an ornament on a Christmas tree, they all said she'd never find another man to love her as much as her husband did, they said and he was such a fine minister, they all said it was a shame she didn't have relatives nearby to comfort her, they all said thank heaven she was such a fine Christian woman who could draw her strength from Christ, they all said the whole ordeal had simply been too much for her to bear poor thing. They all said she'd never be the same again.

3

Ransom, Passing

*And it shall come to pass . . . your young men
shall see visions and your old men shall dream
dreams.*

Acts 2:17

1905

Ransom Tramble had helped his brother Zekiel
build the slave cabin in the heart of Chickenham bottom, so on that January day in 1905—
when Ransom keeled over onto the shelves at
Lincoln Bradley's store in the midst of a-raving and
ranting about how strong he was, knocking down
cartons of snuff, six quart jars of Marveline's honey
and a peach crate full of notions, keeled over from a
stroke that left him paralyzed and with only a holler
for speech—his brother Zekiel's cabin, as crowded
as it was, seemed a fitting place for him to be allowed to die.

And so Ransom was brought there, pulled on a

makeshift stretcher of green cedar limbs and a worn
canvas tent by a team of Ernest Stone Junior's mules
that Ransom himself had trained. In later years
when Samuel Daniel McElroy had outlived everyone his age in both Sugars Spring and Bethel—
which the whites called Chickenham—he'd most
always maintain he cut the cedar limbs himself. In
actuality, at the time his great-uncle was falling,
Samuel Daniel, who was ten going on eleven, was
not even there, but was at Big Mama Mahala McElroy's who lived between Hope and Ozan, and at the
exact time of Ransom's fall, Samuel Daniel was running as fast as his feet could carry him, racing the
Ozan train that passed Big Mama Mahala's field on
its way to Hope every day just as the sun moved
beyond the noon mark.

The land Zekiel's cabin was on had once belonged to Ransom and Zekiel's master, Mr. Benjamin Sugars, who had fathered both Zekiel and
Ransom, and been partial to them over his other
slaves. And even though that partiality was widely
acknowledged, it was a known truth that Benjamin
Sugars' kindness and generosity extended to his
slaves, who at times numbered as many as one hundred, and when he died of a sudden fever in 1854 at
the age of fifty-one, all of his people were, as the
newspaper of the time still attests, "grief-stricken at
the loss of such a kind and benevolent master."

Grief-stricken, too, was the town of Sugars
Spring which promptly closed the doors to all four
stores and went into mourning for two days.

One year and one day later, Benjamin Sugars' widow, Mary Virginia, changed her black mourning suit for a peach-colored day suit and married Harland Tramble who was well mannered but not nearly so well-off as Mary Virginia Reese Sugars, causing many of her relatives to caution her as to Harland's possible motives.

But love is often not tempered with reason, so Mary Virginia Reese Sugars—again according to the newspaper "one of the fairest of women even at her stage in life"—was united in matrimony with Harland Tramble whose first act as the new master was to change all seventy of Mary Virginia's slaves' names from Sugars to Tramble.

Shortly after that, Ransom Tramble, at the time a strapping lad about fifteen or sixteen, ran away—something no Sugars slave had ever so much as attempted to do. It took a two hundred dollar reward and six months of searching before two bounty hunters from east Texas found Ransom doing acrobatic tricks on the backs of horses to the delight of Mexicans, merchants and hardscrabble farmers from Missouri at a circus in Santa Fe.

Harland Tramble paid the bounty hunters, chained Ransom to a cedar post in the barn and ordered the foreman—a good one and loyal—to take the cat-o'nine to Ransom.

Even after such dire punishment it was necessary for Harland Tramble to chain Ransom to a shed on occasion. And in 1863 Ransom, fully grown this time, stole Harland Tramble's bay stal-

lion and headed for the West. But the bay pulled up
lame near Fulton slowing Ransom down, making it
possible for the men assembled by Harland Tramble to catch up with him just as he and the stallion
were getting ready to swim Red River in moonlight.

The next evening under a lilac sky, Harland
Tramble ordered his foreman, again, a strong one
and loyal, to castrate Ransom.

Harland Tramble said he would not have taken
such drastic action, but that Ransom had been
spoilt beyond redemption by his former master Benjamin Sugars. He said Sugars had ignored Ransom's
long-standing habit of slipping out at night, hop-
ping on the fastest horse in the stalls and calling on
girls just coming into womanhood at the Columbus
plantations.

Everyone knew Ransom liked them all. It
didn't matter if they were black as walnuts or shiny
pecan brown. Harland Tramble said no amount of
flogging or chaining had properly tamed Ransom so
there was no other resort.

Soon after the foreman and four other slaves
had carried out Harland Tramble's orders, almost
sooner than Christmas follows Thanksgiving—just
as Ransom was getting healed enough to ride a
mule—Mr. Lincoln freed the slaves. Harland Tramble pronounced at the harness shop that Lincoln
had no power over the Confederacy so who was he
to say what they could and could not own.

That very night, Harland Tramble must have

lifted his head at the moment his horse ran under a low limb of a blackgum as he was galloping home from a lodge meeting. The doctor who examined Harland said he no doubt died instantly of a broken neck which is the exact spot the blackgum whacked him. Everyone in Sugars Spring said maybe someday they'd understand why God had chosen Mary Virginia Reese Sugars Tramble to endure so much grief and sorrow.

Everyone in Chickenham said it was a poor sense of timing. They said if Harland Tramble had met with his accident only a while earlier then Ransom would not have been castrated.

The first thing Ransom did as a free person was help his brother Zekiel, who by the time they were freed had a wife and a baby girl named Mary Kale, build a slave cabin on the eighty acres Mary Virginia deeded to Zekiel, who—like his brother Ransom—was so bright skinned he could have passed for a Spanish explorer. Mary Virginia Reese Sugars Tramble was a good woman, but she saw no need to give land to Ransom as he would, of course, never father children, would never have family to care for.

Ransom and Zekiel stripped the wood and put up the frame of Zekiel's cabin. After they had laid up the logs, chinked them with mud cats and built a cat chimney, Ransom again lit out for the West, taking the bay stallion, the lame leg now healed, the bay stallion that had led Harland Tramble into the

blackgum limb. Mary Virginia declined to offer a
reward for the stallion's return so no one in Hampstead or Harwell County saw or heard a word from
Ransom until he came back seventeen years later, in
1882, with stories that only people who were
touched or children in their gullibility could believe.

Samuel Daniel McElroy, who nearing eleven
was almost man-tall and worked alongside his uncles and aunts in his Granddaddy Zekiel's fields,
didn't believe in haints or hoodoo doctors for the
most part and was cautious about what he'd heard
from the Bible. And even though he'd been told time
and time again by his Grandmama Deborah and his
aunts not to listen to his great-uncle's wild tales, he
sometimes almost believed Great-uncle Ransom's
stories about being a cowboy, about having stolen a
painted pony, or sometimes he said a spotted
horse—a horse so fast it left the whoopin' redskins
eating his dust, a horse that carried him over trails
so narrow he and his horse couldn't have walked
side by side, over trails so high that a horse and man
down below on another trail looked no bigger than
a horsefly, a trail so high that if his horse slipped on
a loose rock they would both have plummeted to
their death in the bottomless ravine.

He wondered if his Great-uncle Ransom really
had killed twenty-six Indians, like he lay claim to
every time he got drunk, selling their scalps to curi-
ous whites, or to wealthy dark-skinned people who
spoke another tongue, for washed and shiny pieces

of gold which he of course had spent all up before returning home on the back of a mule.

Shortly after his return to southwest Arkansas, Ransom sparked The Riot and spent some years in prison, which only served to make him meaner and he continued to cause strife among his own. And for the remainder of his years Ransom got swore at, beat up, cut up, shot at many times, and carried at least one bullet in him. Consequently, no one in all of Bethel—which the whites in neighboring Sugars Spring called Chickenham—would have ever thought it possible that he would die an old man living out his last hours on a sickbed. They were sure he'd be killed in a tavern brawl or in a poker game where he accused someone with a burning temper and a gun of cheating, or maybe his body would cough up out of the swamp one day. They said one reason Ransom was alive was that—except for The Riot of '83—Ransom had always left white folk alone, they said he'd walk two miles to cover fifty feet to avoid gettin' near a white person, they said he had unleashed all his meanness on other drunk and mean niggers. They said look how good he treats his mules, they said he never laid a cruel hand on them or hardly raised his voice, they said look how well he keeps them greased, they said nosirree he never let a one of Ernest Stone's mules get a sore neck.

During those years after Ransom's return, the years that he was drinking and kicking up dust and bragging about his time in the West and stirring up countless fights in Jedidiah Stuart's tavern, and training mules to work in the timber for Ernest Stone Senior and later on Ernest Stone Junior, Zekiel and his wife Deborah were supporting family on the land Mary Virginia Tramble had deeded to Zekiel.

It was rich black land that yielded strong white cotton, but Johnson grass also thrived there, green grass it was, wide as a man's thumb and shiny as pond ice, so the backs of Zekiel and Deborah and Deborah's brothers and the brothers' wives ached deep into the night during planting hoeing and picking but especially during picking time.

In spite of the stubborn grass, Zekiel prospered enough to buy even more land scattered throughout the county and add on a new room and put down a plank floor over the packed dirt one in the old room, giving the children, and later the grandchildren, one room to sleep in while Zekiel and his wife Deborah slept in the big room alone. And Zekiel Tramble took pride in saying that neither his wife, nor his sons' wives, nor any of his daughters, nor any of Deborah's brothers' wives, had ever had to work for a white man—after slavery.

When Ernest Stone Junior's mule dragged Ransom to their place to die, Deborah who was white haired and Zekiel who was bent like applewood pulling toward an underground spring—even though they were only three score and some few years—gave up their bed in the big room to Ransom and crowded into the added-to room with their son Zeke, his wife and several of their children, and their widowed daughter Mary Kale and her two children.

Night after night during the cold wet winter of 1905, Zekiel and Deborah, their daughters and sons, relatives and old neighbors kept vigil in the big room over the withering, wracked body of one who had once been the meanest man in the county.

And on those nights the grandchildren, covered with patchwork quilts and flannel sheeting, sank into the ticking that Grandmama Deborah had made years ago from ducks Ransom and Zekiel had brought down from the sky without wasting a single shot. The grandchildren clumpt their feet together against the soapstone Grandmama Deborah had warmed on the hearth and listened to the sound of sweetgum cracking in the cookstove, to the sound of the north wind sidling through the cracks in the floor, to the sound of their great-uncle hollering and later, when he got the chilblains, coughing like he had a gallon of fluid in his chest, to the creak and sway of their grandmother's rocker. To the voices huddled by the cookstove in the big room.

Sometimes it was the strong, low, swamp-deep voice of Grandmama Deborah—a woman of God—accusing Granddaddy Zekiel of smuggling in spirits and sneaking it down Ransom's throat when her back was turned telling Zekiel, you gonna burn

in almighty hell if you brought such evil into my
house and Granddaddy Zekiel would say in his
voice, as high pitched as a fiddler's reel, law woman
if I could get away with it I would but I couldn't face
the hell you'd put me through here on this earth.
And Grandmama Deborah said doncha be lyin' to
me and Granddaddy Zekiel said I ain't never lied to
you and she said that be the biggest lie of them all
but she said it the way she told the grandchildren
she was gonna whup them within an inch of their
lives when all she gave was a little swat on their
behinds with her tiny hands. Then all the grownups
would laugh and someone would say you two
gonna go right through the pearly gates fightin' and
carryin' on.

Sometimes the voices recounted earlier times
and sometimes the laughter would bounce around
the big room and into the bedroom and make the
grandchildren feel like getting up and bouncing up
and down on their bed and then kicking their legs
out from under them and falling flat on their backs
sinking deep into the feather ticking.

Other times the voices were touched with
something sharp and raw—like ice edged the Arkansas winter rains. At those times the swaying of
Grandmama Deborah's rocker came to a stop with
one distinct creak and in her swamp-deep voice she
told them to hush their voices so as not to disturb
Ransom who was often in a stupor either from
Crazy Sadie's concoction of swamp plants, or from
the whiskey that Samuel Daniel had seen his Grand-

daddy Zekiel work down Ransom's throat in gentle strokes when Grandmama Deborah was at her chores or at prayer meeting.

Or sometimes Deborah and Zekiel's daughter Mary Kale said for them to shush down their voices so they didn't wake the sleeping children, and Grandmama Deborah would agree saying y'all know good and well they don't need to be hearin' bout such things right before dreamin' time.

At those times Samuel Daniel McElroy told the other grandchildren to hush their breathing and told his sister Harriet to hush her thumbsucking and to be very quiet so they could listen for field mice running across their plank floor.

Grandmama Deborah declared that Ransom had gone beggin' for trouble since the day he was born. Other voices agreed and proclaimed that he had been given the most partial of treatment by his first owner and still he was as wild and untamable as a bottom hog, and Grandmama Deborah usually took this time to show them the scars that Emmett Clegg, who had been her master before selling her to Benjamin Sugars, had left on her right arm when she was ten—when all she did was sneak a biscuit as she helped the missus of the house. Some nights they said that if only Ransom had not run off he would have been free and still been a man. They declared that he could have easy as not found him a girl from one of the dozens of Sugars slaves. Just like Zekiel did, they always said.

Then Granddaddy Zekiel said if he hadn't al-

ready taken Deborah to wife he might have run off
with Ransom hisself, he said yessir he just might
would have. Grandmama Deborah said then he
wouldn't of had no children or grandchildren and
Zekiel said well he didn't run away did he so it
wadn' really anything to talk about was it. But he
said *if* he'd run with Ransom they wouldn' of been
caught. And one of the old women's voices said they
all got caught sooner or later and Granddaddy
Zekiel said it wadn' so. He said lots of slaves in Columbus and in Washington had run away and
joined up with Union soldiers and did their own
fightin'. And he reminded them that King Reese—
Safronia Grant's big brother to be exact—run away
the year before Ransom did and never got caught
and to this day in 1905 was probably walking the
world a free man.

An old man's voice that scratched like sandpa-
per said what you talkin' bout man, we all free now
and Granddaddy Zekiel said un-huh, almost like he
was agreeing.

Sometimes they talked about what they called
the Harwell County Riot of '83, or more often they
just said The Riot, which happened before the
grandchildren were born, and which resulted in
death and bloodshed or prison to almost every family in Bethel.

Mostly, the grandchildren knew what it was all
about. They knew that it had to do with a woman
named Ophelia Love who was about the same age

as Samuel Daniel's mother Mary Kale, and who was bright and sightly. They knew the white man Ophelia Love worked for had beat her up when he said she didn't mop the floor but claimed she did. And that when Ransom, riding by, saw her dragging herself home bleeding from every limb and with only one eye open by a slit, he lifted her on his mule and led her to the fields, led her like he was Joseph leading the Virgin Mary, led her to the young men who were hoeing, and at each field Ransom made a speech that set fire to blazing under them.

And while Ransom led the once pretty Ophelia Love home on his mule, the young men—about thirty in number—some of them brothers, and cousins, and many of them would-be sparkers to Ophelia as she was already widowed at nineteen, and some of them mad as hornets, and some of them just plain mean, went home and got their guns and in broad daylight, in daylight so bright the sun pushed all the color from the sky, these young men approached the white man who was out walking his field and shot him as he was running to his horse who was waiting at the end of the row, shot the white man dead as a skint skunk.

The grandchildren knew that someone referred to as the gov'ner sent droves of whites with guns and uniforms and hate in their hearts, whites who killed some of them and put lots of them in prison, including Ransom who hadn't really been on the scene until the second or third day of the riot, but had been the cause of agitating the young men to uncontrollable wrath.

As Ransom lay dying in the big room, the voices brought back the story long passed and tried once more to give reason to it. They said what beat all was that Ransom hisself had no stake in Ophelia Love—he wasn't kin and he certainly couldn't pay court to her, considering his circumstances they always said—so it was befuddling why he simply couldn't have let it be.

They talked about the bullet that still rested in Ransom's back, below and to the left of his right shoulder blade, and Grandmama Deborah said she declared Ransom wore that bullet like a badge even though if it had been one jot or tittle farther over he would have been paralyzed solid for the rest of his life. Grandmama Deborah said it was sin enough for him to be always stirrin' up trouble and fights in those ungodly taverns, but in the case of Ophelia Love, Ransom's rashness had been even costlier to his soul as he had unleashed a flow of blood of young men, good men too, mostly, and with their whole lives before them.

Grandmama Deborah said that she wasn't going to judge him because everybody had sins to be forgiven of, and because the Bible said *judge not unless ye too be judged* but she said someday Ransom would have to stand before his God and account for all the blood spilt that awful week.

Some of the voices said amen. Granddaddy

Zekiel tapped his pipe against the edge of the sweet-gum table and said, in his fiddle voice, that Ransom had just never had the gift of patience, that his brother somehow had never learned the blessings of suffering.

The grandchildren listened and heard and wondered what castration was, agreeing finally that it meant cutting off the whole thing, until Samuel Daniel, who had watched pigs being cut, told them it meant slicing the two balls and squeezing them until the pigs screamed loud enough to be heard for miles.

Samuel Daniel strongly suspected that Great-uncle Ransom had screamed too, that his cry had pierced the elements with his pain, had skidded across the thick green water of Mossy Lake and woke up the alligators in their winter sleep, had darted across the cotton fields like martins before they nest in for the night, and finally his cry had reached the houses and churches in Bethel proper and maybe even had risen, crossing the ridge to Sugars Spring, scattering over the houses of white folks, interrupting their supper prayers.

Although once when Samuel Daniel was much smaller than eleven, and when Great-uncle Ransom was still vigorous even though he was crowding three score, his Granddaddy Zekiel and Great-uncle Ransom were sitting on the porch with the smell of Zekiel's homegrown wafting from their pipes, jawing in their matching voices about what it was to be

a man, Samuel Daniel was sure he remembered
Great-uncle Ransom saying it took a man to stand
there and be sliced like he was no more'n a pig and
not give the world the almighty pleasure of hearing
him scream. Samuel Daniel was sure he remembered
Great-uncle Ransom boasting that he didn't make
no more sound than what Deborah made sneezing
which was so quiet you barely heard it even at the
dinner table prayer.

On that day on the porch, the brothers had
continued to jaw and Granddaddy Zekiel said well
you mighta been somethin' back then but all you is
now is an old nigger with nothin' but a mule barn
for a home. Great-uncle Ransom said nosirree he
wadn' no such thing, he said he could still put many
a man down. He said I'll show you how strong and
pliable this old nigger still be and with that he raised
up off the porch railing where he'd been sitting and
said see that plank?

Samuel Daniel, who was sitting on the steps
breathing in the sweet smoke drifting from the old
men's pipes, sitting unnoticed, trying to whittle a
frog from a dead pecan limb, followed Ransom's
jagged finger to see he was talking about a slat on
the porch roof.

Zekiel let a plume of white smoke curl out of
his mouth and wind round and round on its way off
the porch and said yeah he saw it what about it.
And Ransom said I can jump up and kick that ceiling plank with my foot, kick it hard too. Samuel

Daniel who was very young, not over five, was old enough to know how ridiculous such a boast was—as a matter of fact when he was a very old man spending time sitting on his porch swing brushing his cat, he spoke about how close he came to not even turning his head from the dead pecan limb that he was trying to whittle into something live, how close he came to not seeing.

Samuel Daniel looked up from his pecan-limb frog, and glanced over his left shoulder—he was almost certain it was his left shoulder because he remembered exactly where on the porch steps he was sitting so it would have to have been his left shoulder—in time to see his Great-uncle Ransom walk over to the edge of the porch, so close to the edge Samuel Daniel thought for sure he was going to tumble off backward on top of Granddaddy Zekiel's deerhound, then taking two giant strides and one baby step, Ransom lifted himself feet first as if he didn't weigh no more than a feather, as if a gust of wind had caught hold of him and turned him upside down, as if he were, once again, fifteen years old and doing flips on the back of a horse at a circus in Santa Fe.

Ransom's left foot contacted the plank with such force that it split in half and came tumbling down, the edge of one piece hitting Samuel Daniel on the shoulder, scraping it enough to draw blood and leaving a splinter stuck so deep Grandmama Deborah would have to dig it out with her sewing needle. But Samuel Daniel was in such a state of disbelief and wonder at his great-uncle—who had somehow managed to kick a slat above his head, and then land on his feet without a stagger—that even though Samuel Daniel flinched from the heavy scratch, even though he bled, he didn't cry.

Ransom threw back his head and whacked his leg hard enough to raise pink dust and Granddaddy Zekiel whacked his leg too and said by damn Ransom sure still had the kick of a mule even though he was just an old white-headed nigger and that he spected Ransom better jump on *his* mule and go before Deborah got home from ladies' prayer service and saw her porch ceiling caved in and took her foot to the both of them.

The day of February 12, 1905, began cold and all day the sky spit ice into the thick rain. Then darkness fell, the rain ceased, and the moon rose in the east and hung golden and luminous over Bethel. It was then that Ransom began a kind of hollering that neither prayer, nor Crazy Sadie's concoction from the swamps, nor whiskey which Samuel Daniel was sure he'd seen Grandmama Deborah smoothing drop by drop down Ransom's throat when Granddaddy Zekiel was out splitting kindling, nor even the hoodoo doctor's incantations which the old relatives finally convinced Grandmama Deborah to let them try, could quieten down, his voice getting louder, and louder still when no one could figure out what he was trying to say. An old lady with a broken voice said lawdy sounds like he's howling at the moon that just come up. Grand-mama Deborah said I wonder if he be wantin' forgiveness for his wrongs.

Samuel Daniel lay in the next room, scrunched between his sister and his sleeping cousins, pretending to be asleep himself, hoping for sleep to come and rescue him from the wailing in the next room.

Finally, thankfully, Samuel Daniel felt himself slipping into the shallow stream of sleep where he waded with caution into the deeper river of dreams. He braced his body and lifted his head to keep from being swept over and then pulled under by the whirlpool that lurked in the rivers near Bethel, lifted his head to see the riverbank on the other side, to see a mule, long ribbed and shaggy, under a feeding shed, an old mule with a yoke around his neck. Samuel Daniel chose not to wade any deeper, so he was at the point of turning to go back when the mule lowered its head and kicked so high, so hard, his left hind foot whammed the shed roof, splintering the decayed wood into a thousand pieces, the loudness of the impact jarring Samuel Daniel from his sleep, yanking him from his dreams with such a force he landed, standing upright, on the cold pine floor.

Samuel Daniel was startled that none of the voices in the living room seemed to have heard the sound—so preoccupied they were with trying to calm Ransom for his passing. Samuel Daniel stood there, in his flannel nightshirt, shivering, waging a battle within himself as to whether he should take shelter under the covers or venture to look out the one window in the room.

Samuel Daniel told himself maybe somebody dropped a fireplace log, or that it was probably the toolshed door that sometimes flew open in storms. He told himself that the grown-ups in the next room would protect him from harm. Besides, he told himself, he did not believe in haints anyway so why was he afraid to look. He told himself he was practically twelve and therefore a man who was not afraid of anything.

Samuel Daniel McElroy moved with the silence of a ghost to the one window in the room, pulled back the curtain that Grandmama Deborah had spun with her tiny hands, and saw—what one day he would name to himself—the most awe-filled sight of his one hundred years.

On the porch, just outside the living room, stood Great-uncle Ransom—in his woolen night-dress and barefooted—looking triumphantly at the porch ceiling. His great-uncle whacked his thigh in celebration the same way he had done that day years before when he had brought down the porch roof. Then the old man looked to the west, put two long jagged fingers in his mouth, and whistled so shrill someone in the big room said I swear I heard the kettle whistling when it ain't even on the fire.

Samuel Daniel turned his eyes to where his great-uncle was looking, looking down the road latticed by moonlight and tree-shadow, the road that in daylight was the deep pink of Grandmama Deborah's rosebush but in the dark took on the hue of dried blood.

Samuel Daniel saw a speck moving down the road, a speck no bigger than a flake of snow then growing larger and larger still, until Samuel Daniel could make out the silhouette of a horse, a horse galloping in and out of tree-shadow and moonlight and tree-shadow, a horse that in the moments of moonlight was the color of his grandmama's sun-brightened sheets, the color of his Grandmama Deborah's hair, the color of snow.

And Samuel Daniel knew that he was looking at the pale horse, the giant horse, the Spirit Horse he had heard spoken about many times. Samuel Daniel reminded himself he was almost eleven which was almost twelve and therefore a man and was not afraid of anything even the white horse that roamed the countryside the night before a death, the white horse that could fly across the sky.

Still, even though he was almost twelve and therefore unafraid, Samuel Daniel released his breath in great relief when the horse drew near enough for him to see that it wasn't the big white Spirit Horse after all. It was short and squat and its rump was splashed in color. When it drew to a halt next to the porch, when it flicked its ears, switched its tail and gave a snort of greeting, Samuel Daniel knew this was the Indian pony, Ghebe, that Great-uncle Ransom had told him about. And he had almost believed.

His great-uncle, taking two giants strides and one baby step, leaped onto his pony, his crooked fingers grabbing the short rope around the horse's neck, his bent and bony feet clutching the sway of the horse's back like bird claws.

Great-uncle Ransom threw back his head to make ready for his laugh, the way he did when he won bets or got someone's goat with a trick, or made someone angry enough to kill him.

Samuel Daniel closed his eyes tight to make sure they were truly open. When he opened them again, Great-uncle Ransom had vanished. Standing on the pony was a man with heavy curls, curls the color of molasses, a man with strong, straight fingers, a man wearing only trousers, a man with smooth tight skin, skin that caught the moonlight and sent it shining back.

Samuel Daniel knew as surely as he ever knew anything in his long life that the young man's name was Ransom.

Young Ransom bent down, patted the horse on the neck, whispered in the horse's ear, straightened, tugged the rope to turn his pony west, clicked the side of his mouth and—with the moon at their back lighting the ribbon trail between the stand of cedar on one side, and the fallow field on the other— horse and rider headed west, the horse running swiftly as if the moonlight had miraculously dried the gummed red clay that after each rain sucked and pulled at boots, wagon wheels and horses' feet.

Samuel Daniel, holding back the curtain, watched Ransom ride toward the crest in the road, watched Ransom release the rope and flip—like a hotcake—and land standing on his strong, young hands, Ransom's spotted pony all the time striding as smooth as the gentle glide of a rowboat, watched Ransom point his feet straight to the heavens, hold them there as if pointed in prayer, and then flip, again, to a standing position on the horse's back, his feet landing as firmly as if he stood on solid ground, watched Ransom lift both arms to the sky as the spotted pony—his rope flapping in and out of shadow—carried Ransom over the crest, the crest where the road became black, then became sky.

Samuel Daniel stood there for a long time, his hand locked to the curtain his grandmama spun by hand, stood there as the moon turned from gold to white, then faded and stars emerged, white, bright blue, or burning red.

Samuel Daniel stood there thinking, thinking if he told anyone they'd say he was dreaming, or they'd say he was touched in the head, or they'd say he was outright fibbing, or they'd say he musta been paid a visit from Ol' Beelzebub himself.

Finally, his feet burning from the icy floor, Samuel Daniel turned and walked sleeplike to the bed, thinking this might be the thing they call a stupor.

In the big room, the body on the bed was still

hollering and an old woman said I seen many a passin' and heard wailin' to split my ears but I never heard nothin' quite like this and Granddaddy Zekiel said if we could just figure out what he be sayin', and Grandmama Deborah said maybe if we sing a song.

And Grandmama Deborah started singing in her husky voice. *On Jordan's stormy banks I stand and cast a wishful eye* . . . Samuel Daniel, who wasn't given too much to church songs, thought to go in and tell them that they should go to bed, that their vigil was over, that Ransom Tramble had already passed, that Ransom was just about now most likely crossing Red River, that it was probably from years of habit that Ransom's body still raged.

But Samuel Daniel knew the ones in the big room still thought of him as a child and Grandmama Deborah would scold him for sneaking molasses cookies to bed despite knowin' good and well eatin' just before sleep brought on nightmares.

So, as several of the others in the big room joined Grandmama Deborah on the chorus *we will rest in the fair and happy land by and by, just across from the evergreen shore,* Samuel Daniel McElroy lifted the quilts, slid into bed, pushed his icy feet into the pile of cousins' feet and let his body sink into the comfort of feathers, content to let his elders in the big room wait out the night.

4

Baby, Leaving

That which is far off, and exceeding deep,
who can find it out?

Ecclesiastes 7:24

1934

Baby Turner sat on a cottonwood stump across the road from the line of persimmon trees that marked the beginning of Cora Emery's pasture, her eyes focused on the red clay road lit by a moon that had a sliver missing, a moon the color of a ripe peach. From there she'd be able to spot Wadie White's Packard when it came over the crest where the road ran into sky.

She had waged a battle with sleep all night long as she lay in bed waiting for her grandmama, who was now somewhere in her eighties, and her great-grand, who had laid claim to being one hundred and six for her last four birthdays, to slide into the dreaming part of slumber. Then Baby had called out their names several times to be sure. She wasn't worried about Great-grand because she had lost much of her hearing these last years, but Grand-mama Phoenicia still could hear a mouse scurrying across the floor.

Call me a chicken if you want to I ain't gonna watch them cry and that be that she had said to Wadie the night before at Blue Heaven when he said why couldn' he pick her up in broad daylight after all she was fifteen years old wadn' she, and there wadn' much two old ladies could do to stop her was there so why couldn' he just come driving up when the sun would catch his automobile in its beam causing it to gleam like a spit-shined shoe.

She said I'm gonna pad my bed with feather pillows just like Jacob did and you pick me up at that ol' cottonwood stump in Cora Emery's pasture so's you don't be wakin' them. And just so he didn't argue anymore, she leaned even closer into him and let the rhythm of her body match his like they were one person, like in a truly good song the words match the tune. She stretched her neck up to his face so he'd smell the lilac water she had splashed on her smooth pecan-colored arms and neck. Oh, baby, baby he said, rolling his tongue over his gold tooth, I'll take you anywhere your little heart desires. She gave him a sassy smile and said then take me to St. Louis.

Most folks said she had too much sass for her

own good. But Grandmama Phoenicia always took up for her saying maybe she sass her teacher, and even once she sass the preacher when he tell her to quit squirmin' in church, saying I cain't help it my bottom's asleep and I cain't wake it up, but she don't sass me or her great-grand, and she don't sass God. That's what Phoenicia said at the quilting circle or at bean shellings.

But to Baby she always said lawdy Baby you'd give sass to the devil if you got a chance, and that ain't how you handle the devil. When you see Ol' Beelzebub you gotta stay quiet as a prayer-hush until he slither by.

Once when Baby was smaller and the subject of the devil came up Baby had said Grandmama, what he look like? And her grandmama said he come in all shapes and sizes. Baby said where he live Grandmama, and all but certain he lived with white folks she added do he live Sugars Spring? Phoenicia said yes, he live there. Baby was somewhat relieved for that affirmation, but then her grandmama added he also live in Bethel. For a time, Baby thought if she could live in Texarkana or Hope she wouldn't have to worry about the devil.

Unlike Great-grand Rebekah Sarah who claimed to know the future, claimed she saw it with her green eye, Baby was given to lying awake wondering what the future held, and knowing she couldn't abide it if her future was in Chickenham, hemmed in by the swampy side of Mossy Lake to the south, hemmed in to the north by Sugars Spring, a town where a white woman had no use for you unless you'd hire out to clean her house or do her ironing, a town where the doctor's family gave her grandmama hand-me-downs for Baby and—after receiving the most heartfelt thanks—subtracted the cost of the clothes from her cleaning wages. I ain't gonna clean house for no peckerwood she told Grandmama Phoenicia when Phoenicia said Doc Walker's daughter had inquired about Baby coming to work for her. I ain't gonna iron for no ghostface she said when Phoenicia, who still took in ironing, said what choice you think you got Baby. And Baby said don't get me wrong Grandmama, I'll help you do anything round this house and I'll iron every stitch of clothes you and Great-grand have, but I ain't ironing for Ghostface Walker.

Baby sat on that stump watching the sky bleach from black to slate and she wondered why the sky got light *before* the sun made its appearance. Seemed to her that the sun would have to get there before it shed its light.

She was listening to the peep-peep of a bird in the sweetgum tree behind her, trying to decide if it was a sparrow or a mockingbird, when she saw her Grandmama Phoenicia—even though Baby knew for certain her grandmama was home sleeping like a stone—saw Grandmama Phoenicia's short feet and bowed squatty legs planted right in front of her like she had done many times saying lawdy Baby I swear

I don't know where you got that sass but it's gonna get us all in a heap of trouble. She heard her as surely as she was standing there.

And Baby always said no it ain't, Grandmama, I'm gonna have me a fine life someday. Phoenicia usually shook her head and said I 'low you musta got those dreams of yours when that cyclone whirl you around in the air those few feet. But today, Grandmama Phoenicia just said Baby Baby don't be leavin'.

Baby closed her eyes tight to make Phoenicia vanish. She opened them and looked to the east where she and her mama, Delie, and her brothers were swallowed up by a green cloud that rode in early one morning on the tail of a red sky then turned purple and hit Bethel which the whites and even some of the coloreds called Chickenham before roaring on like a freight train into Sugars Spring. Chewed 'em up and spit 'em out like they was plum pits, her grandmama sometimes said, spit Baby out prac'ly before it picked her up while taking the others all the way across Mossy Lake.

Baby didn't remember her brothers because she was at the age where she had barely learned to walk. She didn't remember her mama, Delie, either, even though sometimes she thought she remembered swirling through the air in her mama's arms but everyone said she didn't.

So even if she did or did not remember that, she didn't remember what Delie looked like. And any pictures of Delie burned the cruel winter of '24, when fire destroyed the house her great-grand had moved into after the same cyclone that took Baby's mama and brothers flattened Rebekah Sarah's house. Flattened it like a hotcake, Grandmama Phoenicia always said. Baby was sure, though, that she remembered Delie's voice and sometimes in uneasy moments—when lightning crisscrossed the sky and thunder clapped so hard it jarred their house, or when the moon hit the trees outside her bedroom window making them look like giant scarecrows, or when she had her window open on a spring night to smell the jasmine and wild roses traveling all the way from Safronia Grant's yard and the screeching of a wildcat caused Baby to pull her quilt over her head—she'd hear a woman's voice, a voice as smooth as the bolt of pink silk that Pleasant Gilbert once had in his store. Baby had ambled over and rubbed her palms against it. But then the woman cutting broadcloth for Phoenicia saw Baby's hands sliding up and down the bolt of silk and said Phoenicia I must ask you not to bring that child with you if she can't behave. Baby still remembered how smooth, slicky almost, that bolt of silk was, but it had also surprised her at how cold the color pink could be.

The voice she heard, the voice that reminded her of silk wasn't cold though. It was warm as flannel, saying don' cry, Baby Girl, everything gonna be awright.

Of course it was Delie, her mama. Who else could it be? No one else had ever called her Baby Girl. In fact, she didn't even know that was her full name until one day when she was about eight or so and Great-grand Rebekah Sarah was again explaining why her real name was Baby, explaining how after the storm Estherlee, Delie's sister, took Baby to raise but Estherlee died the next year of influenza, and Samuel Daniel McElroy, Estherlee's husband, having four kids of his own to raise, relinquished her to Phoenicia—Delie and Estherlee's mama.

Phoenicia took Baby and raised her, refusing to give her another name, even though most everyone in Bethel thought she should be called Rose since they found her walking around Safronia Grant's thicket of wild roses. Baby's mama couldn' find no name that fit that chile so what makes us think we have the power and the right to give her one, Phoenicia said if anyone asked why her grandchild didn't have a real name.

Baby had heard the story many times, but she never tired of it as that was the only time anyone said her mama's name out loud—except for the time Uncle Samuel Daniel had told her she sure to goodness favored Delie, and she could tell by the way he said it that her mama had been a sightly woman. As beautiful as the voice that sometimes floated through the dark.

On this day, as her great-grand finished the

story saying yessir that what Phoenicia said, she tol'
everyone Baby was as good a name as any and that
be your name. Baby said it really be Baby Girl don't
it Great-grand. Great-grand stopped her rocking
and looked at Baby, Rebekah Sarah's brown eye
fogged over with age and her green eye covered with
what looked like pond scum, and said how you
know that chile and Baby said cause my mama tol'
me.

Phoenicia who was listening as she ironed Abigail Huff's lemon-and-sun-bleached sheets in the
other room of the house hollered in and said someone else musta tol' you that cause you wadn' of
rememberin' age when your mama died, someone
else have to have tol' you that, probably your Uncle
Sammy Dan. Don't be so sure Great-grand said,
they be other ways of knowin'. Then Great-grand
continued on with her rocking and looking in the
distance.

Baby sometimes thought it was watching her
great-grand look off into the distance, even after
Great-grand's eyes went bad, that was the first
cause of Baby knowing she had to go away—to
wherever it was that Rebekah Sarah was looking.

The place Great-grand was looking was much
futher away than Cora Emery's which was the first
house you could see after leaving Phoenicia's heading for Sugars Spring. The place Great-grand was
looking was much futher away than Sugars Spring,
too, futher away, even, than Texarkana, although

Baby had never been there and once upon a time thought Texarkana was where Great-grand was looking. But that was when Baby was a child and thought Texarkana and Heaven were probably the same place.

Now, Baby figured Heaven might be St. Louis where there were more silk dresses and lace than you could imagine. Not just lace for trimming dresses either. In St. Louis they even had eating places where coloreds could go, and every single table was covered with lace tablecloths.

Wadie White, who had a car and sweet ways, albeit a wild spirit, was her way to get there. Wadie might be all the things Grandmama Phoenicia said he was, he might be a smooth-tongued soft-souled dandy, and he might be married to a woman in Texarkana like Great-grand said she saw in one of her seein's, a seein' of a sightly woman but very tired, with a young'un on each breast and four more standing in line to drink her milk.

Great-grand said she saw this woman dismayed and in highest agony sayin' Wadie done left me alone to starve with all these kids, now tell me this, tell me how a man can do that to his wife. And Baby said Great-grand ain't no one, not even Prudence Johnson with all her brood got six kids on her tits so that should prove to you this ain't one o' your seein's, it be your imagination gone plumb wild. Maybe you done lost your seein' when you got that scum on your green eye Baby said. She said Wadie's got dreams, he gonna be rich, he ain't gonna stay round here and sell worms like his daddy. Baby said Wadie gonna git hisself a business in St. Louis and he gonna be somebody.

Don't fool yourself chile her great-grand said and then looked off into the distance with her green eye which was often more cloudy than swamp water, looked off as though she could see for miles even though with her eyes more cloudy than swamp water she couldn't make out who people were until they were within touching distance.

Baby had only heard about the power in Rebekah Sarah's eye last fall. They had run out of coal oil so Baby could not see to write her lessons and Grandmama Phoenicia, being plumb give out from oiling the church floor, had fallen to sleep early, leaving Rebekah Sarah and Baby sitting in the blackness, Baby seated at the gumwood table, listening to the rain pelt the tin roof and the old, old woman seated in her rocker, listening to the dark.

Rebekah Sarah began telling Baby about her green eye and what she saw with it. She told about the time in Alabama she saw that her daddy, Baby's great-great, was going to die causin' the earth to get black as pitch in the middle of the day and Rebekah Sarah told her mama what she had seen and her mama chastised her for saying such foolish things. The very next day the moon came between the earth and the sun and it sure enough got black as midnight in the middle of the afternoon, chickens went to roost and cows came up from the fields and that very night white folks hanged Rebekah Sarah's daddy from the horsechestnut tree in the center of town, but not before they castrated him for all to see, saying he had looked at a white woman a certain way.

Rebekah Sarah told how her mama, the mistress's house slave and the master's favorite, turned on Rebekah Sarah, thinking that Rebekah Sarah made it happen because she *said* it would and prevailed upon the master to sell her own flesh and blood. Rebekah Sarah told how she was sold from underneath the same horsechestnut tree her daddy swung from the night they took him, and the folks that bought her brought her from Alabama to New Orleans and then up the river to Fulton where they stood her up on the stump that still was there by the post office and sold her to the Coulters.

Can you believe a woman could axe a man to sell her own flesh and blood Rebekah Sarah said to Baby that night as the rain sounded like drums, can you believe such a thang? Why when they what owned us sold ol' Charlotte here, Rebekah Sarah said—pointing toward Bethel proper with her crooked finger—Charlotte's mama, Jessie Bell, sneak out in the night and brung her back to her bed. And they taken Charlotte back the next day, and the next night Jessie Bell do the same thing. And she do it night after night, the same thing. And Jessie Bell's master, Owen Tibbetts, Mr. Earl Tibbetts'.

grandfather, say to her now Jessie Bell what we gonna do with you, we don't have work enough for your daughter and she's old enough to work now, besides you gets to see her on Sundays if you just quit stealing her every night, and Jessie Bell say Mr. Owen, I gonna work honest and I gonna work hard as long as I gots breath in me, but you gonna have to kill me dead as a fence post if you specs me to stop fetching my baby back. Yes sir, Charlotte herself told me that, and Jessie Bell told me that too many time before she pass.

Rebekah Sarah, spinning her story like a bag swing after being wound round and round and round, said now Jessie Bell say to me, after we was free and both chopped cotton for Zekiel Tramble, that Owen Tibbetts finally threw his hands into the air and say well I'll buy her back then and keep her until she gets fully growed anyway. And before she was fully growed, slavery—as we had come to know it—come to an end, so Jessie Bell didn't have to see Charlotte go off again, lived under the same roof all her days.

Rebekah Sarah quit talking, and the rain quit pounding the tin roof quite so hard. Baby, sedated by the sound of the rain and her great-grand's rocker, by the smell of rain on dry red clay, the smell of the sweetgum table and the rich musty smell of muscadines that Baby and Grandmama Phoenicia had picked that day and would turn into jam to-morrow, began nodding off so she put her head down on the table.

Baby's body jerked to a sitting position. She knew her great-grand was waiting for a reply. She didn't know what her great-grand had asked her, but she knew it was Rebekah Sarah's silence, hanging in the air, that had startled her awake.

Baby was about to say what was that you said Great-grand when Rebekah Sarah's voice, still strong even in the places where it broke, said can you imagine someone could axe to have their flesh and blood sold away, can you imagine that.

N'ome Baby said even though she couldn't imagine many of the things her grand and great-grand talked about. Sure don't understand it myself, don't understand how a mama could do that Rebekah Sarah said, shaking her head in bewilderment. She said I understand Jessie Bell though. I'd rather kill and be kilt than have them take my baby out of my arms. Course we weren't given that choice when Emmett Clegg sold Phoenicia when I hoed the field and her not more'n eight years old, same age as Charlotte be when they sold her. Now I'd lost all sorts of my children to disease and Willie Boy in that wagon wheel accident. And every single one o' the deaths likes to have kilt me, specially seein' it happen before it happen, but nothing scraped down to the bone the way it done that night when I come in and find Phoenicia gone and my green eye hadn' seen it a'tall. 'Fore that, I always be beggin' God to take my seein's away, to strike me blind in that eye and he do for the first time. And I find out it don' help my grief none one way or nother.

Course I retrieved her the day we was freed, walked my feet raw and bleedin' to get to Chapel Hill and fetch her home.

Baby wished her great-grand would quit talking, but something had loosened Rebekah Sarah's tongue. Baby realized then that it wasn't only muscadines she was smelling. She was also smelling some of Miz Melvina's blackberry brandy.

Rebekah Sarah said since that day they sold Phoenicia she had seein's off and on. Sometimes she saw disaster and sometimes disaster came upon her unawares—like the thief in the night that preachers always goin' on bout, she said. She said she also saw James McRae, Cora Emery's husband, dead the day before a railroad car tipped over on him. She said before the cloud ever dipped down from the sky she saw Delie and Baby's brothers blowed away and killed in the cyclone. She said Cora Emery could attest to that. She said Cora Emery was the only person she had told about her seein's since her husband died.

Baby didn't say anything but she thought to herself Great-grand be tellin' her biggest secret to a white woman of all things. On that rainy winter night with no coal-oil lamp and no moonlight to see by, Rebekah Sarah told Baby that for years she hadn't mentioned her green-eyed visions to a single soul—except for Cora Emery—but that she'd seen fit to tell these things to Baby in case Baby one day had a chile with the sight.

Baby froze in the darkness to hear her great-grand, who was by nature the quietest woman she knew, speak almost as long as a sermon and with all the conviction of a preacher, albeit much quieter. Rebekah Sarah said yessir, you just might bear a chile that has the sight since you got my blood. Then she rocked a few more slow easy rocks that sounded like old doors opening.

Baby was on the verge of believing everything Rebekah Sarah told her—even though she knew brandy had strengthened her great-grand's voice and unshackled her tongue—was on the verge of believing it until her great-grand's voice broke the darkness again and said yessir, I'd like to think you'd understand the chile and not go getting the master to sell her down the river.

The darkness lost more of its grip. The sky was now the color of the old gray in Cora Emery's pasture. You better be here soon Wadie White, Baby said aloud. Wadie had said if they got an early start, they'd get to St. Louis that very night. He said he had a cousin that boarded people up and they'd be staying there until he got his dealings under way. Baby said how long that gonna be and he said not to worry her perty little head, he said he'd take care of the money and she could take care of him, and he in turn would take very good care of her, and he'd lick his gold tooth and slide his long fingers down her neck, and futher.

It would be the first time Baby had been any

futher than Hope and only once there. It would be
the first time she'd slept in a bed with a man. But she
wasn't untouched. She had been with Wadie twice
before, once in his Packard and once on the slope of
packed red clay behind Blue Heaven.

But he wasn't the first one. He wasn't the one
who'd brought the blood. The first one was Oliver
Ray Spears, a white constable, who paid a visit one
morning when Baby was sitting on the porch swing
shelling crowder peas, saying he needed to see
Fanny or even Old Rebekah. Ever since Baby had
taken on the first signs of womanhood Phoenicia
had warned her and warned her about the dangers
any white man carried with him and Baby said I
ain't scared of no peckerwood. So when Oliver Ray
pranced up to their porch that morning, Baby reminded herself she wasn't afraid. She wasn't afraid
of anything. Why as a baby she'd been lifted up by a
cyclone, a cyclone that killed her mama and brothers, but not her, a storm that took her across a barbwire fence and placed her in Safronia Grant's wild
rose thicket, and all she got was a few thorn
scratches. But her bravery was tempered when she
remembered her grandmama's caution about the
devil and how he could come in all shapes and sizes.

They ain't here Baby said and she kept right on
swinging, with one leg tucked under the other knee
and her green stone bowl nestled in her lap. Ain't?
he asked. Well, then maybe you can help me he said,
as he swaggered up the steps and stopped so close in
front of Baby she had to quit swinging or bump

against him. She stretched her toe to the porch floor and stopped the swing. And she knew—Grandmama Phoenicia and Great-grand Rebekah Sarah, who moved in with them when her house burned down in '24, had told her enough times—that she should look at the ground any time a white man came within sight, so she forced her eyes down to look at his cowboy boots, brown with gold tips and powdered with a mix of red and black dust, and said I don't know what help I can be.

She felt his eyes hot on her but she kept her eyes on his feet even though she had the urge to throw the bowl of peas in his face or butt her head right at his belly like she'd seen little bull calves do when boys were tormenting them.

Then he said why I declare you ain't no baby no more, why is it they still call you Baby when you already a woman, and Baby just kept staring at his boots and didn't answer even when he said ain'tcha.

Well now I was wondering, Oliver Ray Spears said, and Baby saw his left foot step even closer and she noticed a smudge of chicken manure on the gold toe of the boot. She felt his leg against her leg and he repeated himself saying yessir, I was wondering if the old ladies seen any strange vehicles going back and forth from the bottoms. Mr. Henry's bottom cows is disappearing one by one, and your grannies bein' good niggerladies can probably tell us who the rustlers are.

Baby locked her eyes on his toe, the one

smudged with manure. You hear me little bitch I'm talking to you, Oliver Ray Spears yelled so loud his voice splintered.

Baby lifted her head and looked him dead on with her eyes as dark as ripe mulberries, but she didn't answer. Why you im-pu-tent little black who-ar Oliver Ray Spears said as he grabbed her arm and slung her off the porch and onto the ground. Then he was on her pulling her up by an arm and her hair and hauling her toward the thicket behind her house.

Baby pulled back as hard as she could and tried to dig her feet into hard red dirt, but she still didn't make a sound. She felt the gold-tipped toe of the boot on her belly knocking her to the ground.

He kicked her two more times, kicked the food right out of her belly and stood over her as she heaved the last of it. Then he grabbed her arm and said stand up girl and he pulled her into the thicket and slammed her back against a scrub oak tree. And when he pushed his face up against hers, she could smell the rot of tobacco on his breath, sour enough to match her own and for the second time, she stared him straight on.

Oliver Ray Spears held her tiny wrists in one hand, held them over her head, held them against the rough bark, held them so tight she thought they were going to break like a pulley bone. He used his free hand to unbutton his pants, pull up her green gingham skirt, and yank down and then tear off the

pink cotton bloomers that Phoenicia had hand
stitched for her.

Baby looked at the sky as she felt him thrust
himself into her. She screamed when he tore her, but
he quickly covered her mouth with his big, dirty
hands, hands too that smelled of stale tobacco,
hands big enough to cover her mouth and nose until
she knew he would smother her if she didn't stop
screaming. She closed her eyes hoping to hear her
mama's comforting voice telling her everything was
going to be okay. But all she heard was Oliver Ray
Spears grunting like a hog rooting for his slop.

When he was done—which took only a few
seconds—he left her saying I'll be droppin' by another time when the old ladies is at the sewing circle, or the next time that niggerlovin' McRae
woman takes them to the doctor. And Baby knew,
then, Oliver Ray Spears had planned this abomina-
tion all along, and no matter how much she had
looked down, how much she had avoided looking
him in the eye, it wouldn't have made one speck of
a difference.

And she knew the voice, Delie's warm flannel
voice that had comforted her through her childhood, had taken leave and that from now it was up
to Baby to find her own way.

She drew water from the well and washed the
blood from her skirt. She threw water between her
legs. Then she took their shovel and buried her un-
derpants behind the smoke shed. She went to the

front yard, and finding the stone bowl had somehow survived the flight across the porch, gathered
up the peas scattered over the yard and was on the
porch shelling peas when her grandmama and
great-grand came home.

Phoenicia said law girl it taken you all this time
to shell them little bit of peas? But Rebekah Sarah
said Phoenicia leave the chile be.

Later, when her Grandmama Phoenicia was in
the kitchen cooking up the peas and hog jowl for
their supper, and Baby and Rebekah Sarah were sitting on the back porch watching the sun sink behind
the cypress trees of Mossy Lake, Rebekah Sarah
said I been wonderin' if that constable come round
when we not here and Baby not wanting to upset
the old ladies said n'ome. But she knew Great-grand
recognized that to be a lie.

The next day Baby was on the front porch
again when Oliver Ray Spears and the high sheriff,
David Ben Sugars, who Great-grand and any coloreds worth their salt proclaimed to be an honest
and upright man, came to talk to the two old
women about the rustlers. Oliver Ray Spears acted
like the utmost gentleman, tipping his hat to Baby
and taking it off when her great-grand came to the
screen door. Baby didn't know if it was because
Great-grand and Grandmama Phoenicia were home
or because the high sheriff was with him that Oliver
Ray Spears had taken on the airs of a gentleman,
nodding his head almost like a bow as he greeted

the ladies and saying yes ma'am and no ma'am at intervals.

But she knew he'd return. She knew she wasn't safe even in the confincs of her own house, she knew she had to rush up her plans to get out of Bethel, out of this place called Chickenham.

At first she thought maybe the preacher's son, Jeremiah Parsons, would be her way out—her salvation. Brother Parsons lived in Delight but he held a revival in Bethel every June and the last two years he'd brought his son along as song leader. Jeremiah was just a few years older than Baby. He carried himself tall and proudlike and his hair was molded in perfect waves and everybody said he was sure as shootin' going to make a grand preacher just like his daddy. And it was obvious that his daddy had done hisself proud, dressing in silk suits and shoes that gleamed, and driving a car as long as any two cars in Chickenham.

So when the revival started shortly after Oliver Ray Spears' visit, Baby set about to entice Jeremiah and began imagining herself as a preacher's wife in a big congregation in Texarkana or maybe even Little Rock, sitting every Sunday on the second row from the front with a dotted-swiss dress edged in ruffles, and a fan that folded and spread out like a butterfly. And she'd lift her voice in praise louder than anyone and outsway them all, 'cause after all she was married to the preacher wadn' she.

When Jeremiah stood before them and led them, singing *some glad morning when this life is o'er, I'll fly away,* she'd steel her eyes on his face and just as his eyes met hers and became snagged there for a few seconds, she'd give a slight smile, one that, somehow she knew, had promises behind it.

Night after night, as Brother Parsons traipsed about the stage talking about how Hell was reserved for the unrighteous but the righteous had a crown waiting for them in Heaven, and that drinking and dancing and such as what occurred in Blue Heaven was definitely in the unrighteous category, Baby sat on the second row by the window that brought just enough breeze to carry the scent of jasmine oil she had worked through her hair to Jeremiah sitting on the front row.

And night after night she walked up to him afterward and said you sure can sing, and Jeremiah said why thank you, or she'd say I sure do like that song you picked tonight and he'd say thank you sweetie. Then on the last night, just as they gathered to go into the church, Baby slipped him a note that said I sure wish you could come back to Bethel all by yourself and we could talk about the gospel. She said that partially because she wanted to know more about the salvation that had not yet been visited upon her, and because she knew a preacher's wife had to learn much about such things. And because his eyes when they looked back at her made her feel like she had just come into a warm room in the middle of winter.

She slipped him the note, on brown grocery paper, and it wasn't five minutes later—after Jeremiah had led them in singing *are you washed in the blood of the lamb*—that Brother Parsons announced that Jeremiah was taking himself a wife, a wonderful Christian girl from Delight and he wanted the congregation to pray for them that they be faithful in the Lord and that they be fruitful and multiply.

Two nights later, Jeremiah drove all the way from Delight, drove up to Baby's house at nine o'-clock, knowing good and well it was past the old ladies' bedtime, on the pretense of returning some of Phoenicia's canning jars and said how good everything had been, the pickled peaches most especially. Then he asked Baby if she wanted a ride in his car.

They parked down by the swamp. He talked low and sweet to her the whole time he was touching her, touching her as gentle as one rubs a kitten, telling her she was about the prettiest thing he ever did feast his eyes on, and when he entered her, she groaned out of sheer pleasure and he groaned in a delight that she thought surely must be love.

Then he told her he was getting married the next week and he was going to do his best not to commit this grievous sin anymore.

Baby took to waiting until the old women were asleep and then going to Blue Heaven, and that's where she started hearing and then singing songs other than the ones about Jesus that she learned at

church or the ones about waiting for freedom that
Grandmama Phoenicia had sung to her since she
was a child.

And that's where she met Wadie who told her
about a place called St. Louis with a train station
that could swallow up all of Bethel proper. A place
that sounded much more exciting than Heaven or
any of the places in her grandmama's songs, even if
it wasn't the place Great-grand looked to. A place
with stores that sold nothing but fur coats that kept
women warm and looking like queens. A place with
store after store brim full of already made silk
dresses—not just one bolt in the back of the store
that she was forbidden to touch.

Baby reckoned she was lured to that bolt of silk
in the way Eve had been beckoned by the fruit—the
fruit her grandmama and all the preachers said was
a big red apple but her great-grand stubbornly insisted was a ripe orange persimmon.

The sky lightened even more but was now
trimmed in pink, hinting at rain, rain that would
please her grand and great-grand as their garden
was thirsty. She wanted to tell them both good-bye.
She wanted to feel Grandmama Phoenicia's big soft
body, a body that smelled like rich, black, newly
turned earth, swallow her up and surround her one
more time. She wanted Great-grand to sit in her
rocker, look out into the distance and say it's alright
chile, I done looked down that road you headin'
and it be good.

But she knew in reality Grandmama Phoenicia would wail and wail, and she knew Great-grand would retreat even deeper into her quiet, so she left them a note on grocery-sack paper saying she loved them but she couldn't stay there even though she loved them dearly and truly and with all her heart, saying she was smothering here in Chickenham, saying she was dying as surely as the old grape vine out in their backyard, saying it must be her lot in life to ride the wind where it takes her. Saying she'd send them money as soon as she could and that indeed she loved them.

The single sound of the sparrow was by now joined by a boisterous chorus and Baby thought about picking out the different sounds like Uncle Sammy Dan had taught her to do when she was a little girl. She had just named a redwing blackbird— or a mockingbird—when the sun rose up over the crest where the red clay road first touched the sky, the sheer beauty and promise of it almost taking Baby's breath away.

A split second later, Wadie's car, followed by a ribbon of red swirls, lunged over the same crest. Baby let out her breath, stood up, smoothed her dark blue skirt with her hands the color of pecans, and looked back at the gray two-room house sitting on its stilts to make room for the rising of the swamp. She knew the old women would be waking soon and the pain they were facing caused her eyes to brim.

She turned around, lifted her chin, and pulled the gathers in her skirt. By the time Wadie could see her, she was smiling her smile that Wadie always said surely at one time belonged to some long-ago queen. Hey Baby he said as he leaned over and opened the door.

From now on my name is Jasmine, she said. Jasmine Rose.

Cora Emery was the only person black or white who actually saw Baby leaving with Wadie. She was down on her knees, thinning her iris garden by digging them up by the roots to transplant or give away, when they flew by, churning dust that floated onto Cora Emery and her garden, Baby sitting close to Wadie, looking back in the direction they came from as if she expected her grandmothers to come thundering down the road at the speed of a car to overtake them, give Wadie the dressing down of his life and order Baby to get back home at once. Or at least that's how Cora Emery interpreted Baby's posture later when she had the time to think about it. At the time, though, she thought Baby was probably just slipping off for a day's excursion, and Cora Emery said to herself that girl's gonna be a handful for Rebekah Sarah and Phoenicia before she's grown.

Cora Emery finished her digging. Then she ate a breakfast of last night's cornbread, spread with muscadine jelly, drank a glass of buttermilk, tidied up her small mess, hung the damp tea towels across the clothesline in her backyard and drove her old Model T into Sugars Spring to buy lard and flour for the pies she'd promised Little Jewel Sugars she'd make for her sister Daisy Flowers' shower.

She ran into Little Jewel at Pleasant Gilbert's store and Little Jewel convinced her they'd have quite a nice time if they did the baking together at Little Jewel's house, assuring Cora Emery that she had plenty of eggs, syrup and dried fruits and that the frost had ripened the persimmons on her tree— the transplanted tree that Cora Emery had given Little Jewel and David Ben for a wedding present— so they could bake persimmon pies as well. I could sure use your expertise, Miz Cora Emery, Little Jewel said, even though Little Jewel was already at her young age reputed to be a fine pie-maker. Cora Emery consented, only if Jewel would let her provide the lard and flour, and some of the persimmons.

So Cora Emery wasn't there to hear Phoenicia's wailing when she discovered the note, wailing that was finally quieted by the calming effect of Rebekah Sarah's, the same silence that Rebekah Sarah used when she was the mama and Phoenicia was the girl. Nor was Cora there to see Oliver Ray Spears drive by in his dark green pickup on his way to the old ladies' house, assuming the old ladies would be at their Thursday morning prayer circle, not knowing it had been postponed until Friday, not knowing Baby and Wadie had already passed through Delight and Arkadelphia by the time Oliver Ray Spears arrived there to take his pleasure with Baby.

And Cora Emery wasn't there to see that somebody who might have been rustlers did *not* come by at any time that day. She did get home before the rain, in time to get her tea towels off the line before the sprinkle became a downpour.

No one missed Oliver Ray Spears until he didn't show up at supper even though his wife Betty Janine had reminded him she'd be fixin' chicken-fried steak which was his favorite. When he still wasn't home by midnight, Betty Janine went knocking on the screen door of David Ben Sugars' house, waking not only Sheriff Sugars but his wife and their three small daughters. David Ben Sugars told her he wouldn't be worried if he were her, that he suspected Oliver Ray was off checking out some leads they'd gotten on stills. Truth is, David Ben suspected that Oliver Ray was philandering with one of the wives of the night-shift workers at the cement plant in White Bluff, so he told her not to worry and Little Jewel, tying her plaid flannel robe around her, said Betty Janine honey why don't you have a slice of persimmon pie and some coffee to calm your nerves. And Betty Janine said but the only time I can be sure he gets home on time for supper is when I have chicken-fried steak.

When Betty Janine showed up again at David

Ben and Little Jewel Sugars' the next morning, just as they were sitting down at the breakfast table, saying Oliver Ray still hadn't come back home, saying I know some harm has come to him, I know it as sure as I know my name, David Ben figured she just might be right, so he got up from the table and started putting on his gun belt. Little Jewel said you at least have to eat, and you too, Betty Janine. And at the breakfast table, Little Jewel Sugars offered up a prayer for David Ben's safe return. Then she remembered Oliver Ray Spears and asked for his safe return too.

Later that afternoon they found Oliver Ray Spears' abandoned truck in the shallow waters of Mossy Lake, its two front tires sucked down into the swamp, snake green water crawling as high as the seat in the cab. But there was no sign of Oliver Ray Spears. Since the water of Mossy Lake marked the beginning of Harwell County even though the road landing itself was Hampstead County, David Ben Sugars called in Omar Hicks, the sheriff of Harwell County, who called in special investigators since it was after all a man of the law who had disappeared.

Cora Emery had to tell her story again and again to David Ben, and to all the other sheriffs and lawmen, and investigators from Hope and Texarkana and as far away as Little Rock.

In spite of a thorough investigation of every possibility, of which there were many, Oliver Ray

Spears' body was never found, so folks in Sugars
Spring and Bethel passed around their own stories
until they became set enough to call it the truth.

In Sugars Spring, they said that Baby, the tornado baby or the cyclone baby or the storm baby,
was as wild as they raise 'em in spite of the fact that
she was reared by old Phoenicia, as good a Christian as you can find among coloreds. They said that
probably Baby was sleeping with every man in
Chickenham and what few white men she could
lure by prancing around in front of them when
they'd imbibed too much. Otis Marcum who talked
through a mouthful of rotten teeth said Oliver Ray
had told him not two days before he disappeared
that the prissy young colored girl called Baby had
offered herself to him but he turned her down flat
out. Otis said I tol' that boy time and time again to
quit carrying all his money on his person. Otis said
Baby, not getting any money from Oliver Ray by
trying to sell her body, then told Oliver Ray she had
certain information about the rustlers and that she
knew the whereabouts of two new stills, so—according to Otis—Oliver Ray was heading down to
see her that morning, and even though he fully expected she'd ask for money in exchange for such
information he intended to pry it out of her if he had
to pull teeth.

The men in Sugars Spring sat under the sycamore at Pleasant Gilbert's store until the cold drove
them inside to sit around the potbellied stove in the

corner of the store. They said no doubt Baby and
Wadie White, her accomplice, had lured Oliver
Ray to the swamp with the promise of information and then had killed him and probably
weighted his body down with automobile parts,
that his body was probably eaten by gators or
mired in the muck, stumps and stubble of Mossy
Lake and probably would never be coughed up.
The men packed tobacco hard into their pipes and
said Oliver Ray should have made sure he had his
gun cocked and loaded, that he obviously had not
realized a fifteen-year-old nigger girl could perpe-
trate such a deed, that he was too trusting for his
own good.

The women in Sugars Spring stood around in
kitchens stirring pots and fanning the heat from
their pale faces, or they sat in living rooms their needles flitting in and out of flower baskets or rose
vines and said it broke their hearts because Rebekah
Sarah and Fanny were two of the finest coloreds
they knew and the two old women had already had
many crosses to bear. They said Rebekah Sarah had
lived long enough to see all her children—except
Fanny—dead and buried, they said Fanny had lost
her daughter, wasn't her name Delilah or Delia, and
several grandkids in the cyclone of 1920, and then
the year after the storm she lost her daughter, Elsie
something, or was it vice versa, to the outbreak of
influenza.

Or they sat around quilting frames, needles

darting up and down on the chalk line of the pattern as they tried to recall how Fanny's sons had died. They said one had died in a logging accident, and another came back after the war and then took off shortly after saying he was going back to Paris and he didn't mean Paris, Texas, and that Fanny had received word just last year that he died of pneumonia in France. No that had to be her grandson, the one who fought in the war.

Abigail Huff was sure two of them had died of smallpox, and Jewel Sugars thought it might be three. Someone said she was sure Fanny had only one or two sons and they had died of whooping cough and that Fanny's daughter who got blown away by the storm was the one with three sons.

Abigail Huff who sat as if she were still corseted said well maybe Fanny's daughter got blowed away in the storm because she had her daughter, at least, out of wedlock and she was sleeping with a white man, so the cyclone baby had in her the seeds to be evil. And someone said then why didn't God just take that baby girl in the storm, why didn't He just take the whole family, and not leave her around to bring an end to Oliver Ray who was a fine husband and father, not to mention the grief she brought to Betty Janine, and Little Jewel said that God moved in mysterious ways His wonders to perform.

Montgomery Sugars, David Ben's mama, who had too much work to do on her Jersey farm to be attending quilting bees but had succumbed this time to her daughter-in-law's invitation for persimmon pie said goldang it, y'all talking bout Oliver Ray like he was a saint and I tell you for a fact he was a bigger sinner than any nigger you'd find in all of Chickenham. And Jenny Hughes said don't you think you're exaggerating just a bit Miz Montgomery.

Montgomery thought a minute before amending her statement to say Oliver Ray was a bigger sinner than *all* the niggers in Chickenham put together.

Out of deference to Little Jewel, no one threw up to Montgomery that she should be expected to take *their* side since she was a nigger lover who had been known to sit down at the same table with them, and that it was attitudes like that which caused her girls and her son, David Ben, to be so wild even after they were grown and that she should be grateful to God that her son at least— thanks to the fact that he married Little Jewel— was now a fine husband, a fine sheriff *and* a fine Christian. To keep from losing their poise, they jabbed their needles up and down, up and down until Little Jewel suggested they take a break and have some persimmon pie from the tree that was a gift from Miz Cora Emery—who never attended quilting bees saying they made her feel confined—a tree she and David Ben had transplanted the year they got married.

*   *   *

David Ben Sugars—who was never given to
many words—carried Oliver Ray Spears' disappearance heavy in his heart because David Ben had
been the one who enlisted Oliver Ray in the mis-
sions of catching rustlers and finding and demolish-
ing stills, busting them up so they'd never be in
operation again. David Ben prided himself on his
knowledge of the woods, the bottomland, and of
Mossy Lake, and he had a working relationship
with the coloreds, so when he was alone he up-
braided himself for not being with Oliver Ray that
day.

It hadn't helped the investigation that it rained
in torrents the evening of the day Oliver Ray disappeared, washing away any imprints rustlers or anyone else would have made with their tires.

David Ben talked to Cora Emery time and time
again, since she was the last white person on the
road before Chickenham began, and since she spent
so much time outside in her garden, or just sitting
on the front porch steps, she must have seen something, if not that day, something around that time
that might be a part of what was nagging at him.
Cora Emery had, by coincidence, been at his house
with his wife, making pies for Daisy Flowers'
shower. And try as she might, drawing her wide
forehead into a furrow of thought and searching as
deep as she could, Cora Emery could only tell David

Ben that she saw Baby and Wadie leave town shortly after dawn, and Baby was looking back and Wadie was driving like he was running from a brushfire. But she had not seen Oliver Ray Spears' truck go by earlier, or later, or anytime at all.

Betty Janine said Oliver Ray Spears had left home before sunup, around four o'clock, at least by five o'clock, and then she finally admitted he hadn't been home at all the night before she reported him missing, but he had told her he would be out all night watching a still, so she didn't get worried until he didn't come home for his chicken-fried steak dinner Thursday night.

David Ben didn't know of any still Oliver Ray was watching, although they did find a pint of white lightning, whiskey clear as the water at Sugars Spring, in Oliver Ray's truck. Maybe he had made a buy and the moonshiners had cottoned on to him and did him in. But David Ben doubted that, since he strongly suspected the moonshine ring to be composed of several coloreds he knew and a white woman from McNab, and while he didn't think any of them were worth a plug nickel, he didn't think any of them were the murdering kind. Still, he questioned each of the suspected moonshiners and found he believed their denials.

Something inside, something he couldn't name, had planted a seed of doubt that Baby and Wadie had indeed robbed and then killed Oliver Ray and planted him God knows where. But David Ben

knew he had to keep looking for the truth. David
Ben went back to Rebekah Sarah and Phoenicia
who had given him nothing useful the first time.
Phoenicia had cried and carried on about her baby
being gone, and said she couldn't believe they'd
think Baby would do such a thing, and Rebekah
Sarah stared and looked out the window and
said she'd seen nothing, that she was in fact near
blindness.

The last time he went, Rebekah Sarah sat in her
rocker facing the back of the house, staring out toward the swamp with her different-colored eyes,
seeming not to hear the questions he asked. But
Phoenicia had gained her composure and said she'd
be of any help she could. She offered him some
peach-leaf tea which she assured him was good for
any ailment and David Ben said no thank you just
the same but he didn't drink tea. She offered him a
seat but he said no thanks he'd stand and she knew
he was being a gentleman since there were only two
chairs in the room and Rebekah Sarah occupied one
of them.

Phoenicia stayed standing too even though
Sheriff Sugars said several times and nicely for her
to sit, stayed standing with a sharp winter sun
bouncing through their house and out the back window, flooding light on the green swamp. She stood
there swaying as if to keep balance and told the high
sheriff that yes indeed she had seen Oliver Ray
Spears' truck go by, but first another truck had gone

by in the middle of the night and she watched it until it was out of sight, to where the road turned to keep from going into the swamp. And yes, she knew exactly what color it was, it was black as tar, and it had a Texas license plate, and no she didn't know the number of course since she couldn't read numbers in the dark and that truck disturbed her sleep so she stayed awake the rest of the night.

But she said she could assure the high sheriff that wasn't all she had seen. She said around midmorning the constable's truck come along, and it was shortly after that the black truck come barreling out of there, but it didn't have no cattle on back, or maybe it did, but it sure was flying, flying so fast that she turned to her mama and said Mama whoever drivin' that truck must be in a powerful hurry. She said axe my mama didn't I say they'se runnin' from trouble sure as I know my name.

David Ben knelt down in front of Rebekah Sarah who claimed that day to be one hundred and twelve years old and said Miz Rebekah Sarah, you hearin' what Miz Phoenicia's telling me? Rebekah Sarah said I'm hearin' it and it be the truth.

Still, something about the way she kept staring out into the swamp with a brown eye as clear as glass rinsed in borax and a green eye that looked like it had spider webbing across it bothered him, so he said you sure you're tellin' me the truth now Miz Rebekah Sarah?

Rebekah Sarah kept staring out the back window, staring at the swamp, shafts of green light glowing where the sun coursed through the cypress trees. David Ben had just shifted the weight from his knee to his other foot in order to stand when Rebekah Sarah looked deep into his eyes with not only her brown eye but with her green eye too which seemed, strangely, to be the one she was really using, and in a voice that was raspy but still sounded strong and deep said Baby didn't kill Oliver Ray Spears, but I can tell you he be dead, as dead as that mouse over there's gonna be when our cat gets done foolin' with him.

David Ben Sugars knew that Rebekah Sarah had said all she was going to say. He thought, for a minute, that he'd ask Phoenicia some more questions, poke holes in her story. How did she know it was a Texas license plate—if it was too dark to read the numbers, how could she read Texas? If she watched the truck go all the way to the swamp she would have had to have been in the kitchen, and that was where Baby slept, so why hadn't she noticed Baby was gone, or if she was awake the whole time after that, like she claimed, then why didn't she hear or see Baby leave?

David Ben Sugars didn't believe a word of Phoenicia's story although she stopped swaying and planted her feet firmly and stood like she was a big strong tree that a wind couldn't budge the second time she recited it. He did, however, believe Rebekah Sarah when she said that Baby and Wadie hadn't killed Oliver Ray Spears, and he believed Rebekah Sarah when she said Oliver Ray Spears was dead. He suspected he had come as close to the truth as he wanted to get, so he finally let the matter die—after all, there was no body, Betty Janine had moved back to McNab to be near her folks so she wasn't around to be looked after or pitied, and he had his hands full being on the lookout for Bonnie Parker and Clyde Barrow who were purported to be in the area, so he let the matter drop.

Talk of the disappearance of Oliver Ray Spears drifted around Bethel and Sugars Spring for a few years more and then moved aside as a flood, another tornado, a drought, a shoot-out in Blue Heaven, a lynching, and the task of simply having enough food to stay alive came to the forefront of peoples' lives in both Bethel and Sugars Spring, so five years later, in 1939, when Tump Dyer and Bobo Hughes, two boys from Sugars Spring on their first fishing trip without grownups, came upon a hollow log in the bottoms and, deciding to crawl through it, dug out the dirt with the strong ends of poles and crawled into the log, crawled onto a skeleton, no one made the connection at first that it was Oliver Ray's remains. Tump and Bobo thought some animal had crawled in there and died and probably wouldn't have mentioned it to anyone until it dawned on them—while they were in the

middle of the log—that the animal had been wearing clothes and a rusty watch. They scooted out of
the log, dropped their fishing poles and their worm
buckets, and Tump Dyer's straw hat came off but
he didn't bother to stop and retrieve it.

Saverne Dyer, Tump's mama, fetched David
Ben Sugars who was still the sheriff. Betty Janine
refused to identify the clothes or the watch, refused
to even look at them, and Sheriff Sugars was occupied with trying to keep the soldiers on bivouac in
the area from forgetting that they should behave
like gentlemen even if they were practicing for war,
and with consoling his wife Little Jewel whose baby
sister Lily had recently pulled a disappearing act
herself, leaving her husband—the song leader at the
church—for a soldier she met over a Coke at
Homer's Service Station and Cafe.

So what is known today as Dead Man's Hollow, just across from the old Emery place, most
probably should be called Spears' Hollow, though
others say the bones could have been those of a
tramp who got off the train, wandered into the hollow and crawled up in the log for shelter.

Rebekah Sarah, who claimed at times to be one
hundred and fifteen, died in her silence, having gone
totally blind and almost deaf a few years before. She
never talked to anyone about that day—except for
the one piece of truth she told the sheriff—not even

telling her story to Cora Emery, not because she didn't trust her, but because Rebekah Sarah was well acquainted with the awful burdens of truth.

Phoenicia didn't live to be as old as Rebekah Sarah, but she almost made it to one hundred. It was after her mama died, and after they'd found the remains of what might have been Oliver Ray Spears, that Phoenicia ended her long silence as she sat on her porch in her rusted iron-bottom chair reflecting back on that fall day in 1934, the day that had looked to be fluffy and pink on her waking, the day that she had begun singing as she dressed *Lord lift me up and let me stand by faith on Canaan's happy land,* but the song had stopped when she entered the kitchen and spotted the scrap of brown paper sack on the table, then she spotted Baby's empty bed.

Phoenicia said it seemed to her the pain on that scrap of paper was like all the other losses, all the other deaths rolled into one. She cried so loud she was certain she had frightened the swamp frogs. Then Rebekah Sarah told her to shush her wailing or it'd waken and disturb the dead. And Phoenicia hushed just like she was still a child. She had never before heard anger in her mama's voice, but that morning Rebekah Sarah's voice was weighted down with that anger the way lead weighs down a fishing line, weighted down as she said don't you know cryin' ain't gonna 'complish nothin'.

When Oliver Ray Spears came driving up to

their house, Phoenicia remembered she was sitting in the very chair she now sat in, and she turned to her mama and said it seem like he be droppin' by every time we turn around. And Rebekah Sarah said he won't get what he came for this time. She looked into her mama's face and saw all the knowledge in the world swirling in that green eye of hers. It was that exact moment, Phoenicia said, that she knew what her mama meant and what it was they were going to do.

And sure enough, Phoenicia said with a hint of a laugh but it might have been a nervous laugh, that very day, can you believe, the constable strutted up to the porch and said you old ladies not at church? And then he said where's Baby they's something I gotta ask her. It was then, Phoenicia said, that I be close to tears again but Mama find her voice and say Baby be coming home so why don't you have some of our peach-leaf tea and wait for her. Constable Spears said well I don't drink tea and Rebekah Sarah said then would you have some of my brandy I keep on hand only for medicinal purposes of course. The constable spit a plug of tobacco over the edge of the porch, the tobacco splattering brown on the pale blue chicory flowers. He said well I tell you I been havin' a bout with sum'n so I'm just gonna take y'all up on that offer.

It was then, Phoenicia said, that Rebekah Sarah turned to her and said Phoenicia, go get the constable here some of my medicine—and make sure he get the *good* stuff, the good stuff being their name for certain powders that Crazy Sadie gave to Rebekah Sarah.

Phoenicia went into the kitchen, poured his brandy into a jelly jar. She took the powders of Crazy Sadie—taken from the buckeye and night-shade and requiring great care in measuring lest someone take too much in other circumstances—and dumped a mess of it into that jelly jar. She took it to the constable who had plopped down on the front porch swing like he owned it. Rebekah Sarah sat in a cane-bottom chair and Phoenicia stood next to the swing watching him swig that brandy down like an old drunk. He said he needed to ask Baby some questions about the goin's-on in Blue Heaven. I'll take that girl of yours down to the swamp so we won't trouble you ladies, he said. Then you could tell his head started to spin, spinning so that his eyes almost closed in midsentence. She and her mama had thought to say later—to explain Oliver Ray Spears' demise—that it seemed like he had a stroke causing him to fall and it was just bad luck that his head hit the big rock they used for a doorstop.

And on that hot August afternoon in 1941, when Phoenicia finally broke her silence, telling her story to only one listener as she sat on the rusted iron-bottom chair on her porch, she almost told the story that way. After all, it had the sound of a made-up story to both her and the listener even though she said over there in her shed was the shovel that she and her mama used to hit him over the head.

Phoenicia said she'd've stayed as mute as ol'

Aunt Lula, but she got to thinking about Baby—who had never returned but just might—and she wanted at least one person to know that Baby Girl was as innocent as a newborn Hereford and probably didn't know until this day that Oliver Ray Spears was as dead as the shovel that kilt him.

When Phoenicia got to the part where Oliver Ray Spears, afflicted with a stroke causing his head to swirl, fell to the porch, she paused as if she herself were lost in the swirl of her words. She seemed to be considering if this was where to end, to cease talking. But by now it seemed she was drawn into the whirl of her story, drawn to the memory that had collected cobwebs and dust sitting, unshared, in her mind, so there was no use trying to pull out.

Pointing a finger to the field, Phoenicia said they decided to hide him instead so they dragged his body to his truck. She paused as if all these years later she was still tired from pulling him by his feet. She said they tried to get him in his truck but they were simply too old to lift a dead body that high. She said so my mama and me hitch up our ol' mule Cornelius and tie his body to it like he be a plow and the mule—thank Jesus—was in a cooperative spirit that day and we drag it out to the hollow to bury it. Lawd that body be heavier than any sack of cotton I ever dragged. Mama said evil still be heavy even if it be dead. When we got there we had plumb forgot to bring along the shovel. Then Mama say we gotta move his truck down by the swamp so no one will know he was ever at our house, then we can worry bout his body. So we left the constable, lashed behind our mule, and went back to hide the truck. Phoenicia paused and straightened her back as best she could, as if it would give her strength to trudge from the field back to their house and climb into Oliver Ray Spears' truck. She said when they got to the truck Rebekah Sarah told her to drive since her eyes were still good. Only problem with that, Phoenicia said, lacing her words with laughter, be that I don't know how to drive and I cuss myself for ridin' in automobiles all those years and never learnin' how. So I turns the key and starts pushin' with my foot and movin' that stick around like I seen folks do. The truck lurch and the motor groan but it won't keep goin', but I keep movin' the stick and pushin' them pedals on the floor. Finally that truck start rollin' on its own, rollin' down the road toward the swamp where we was gonna take it anyway—so it seemed destined. And maybe even blessed.

But we got ourselves in a pickle cause come time to stop that truck no amount of jerking that stick around would stop it, and before you know it there we was in the swamp with that green water snaking in under the door.

Phoenicia, shaking her head in amazement, said now don't axe me how we got ourselves out of that cab and onto the roof—cause it done escape my memory—but we was sittin' on that roof when

Samuel Daniel come lumberin' along in his wagon, sittin' on the roof of that ol' truck lookin' like baby birds stranded in a nest, that's how Samuel Daniel put it when he came—just like our Savior, or least-wise like Noah—to save us.

Phoenicia stopped, and a startled look crossed her face, a look like she got when called awake by the preacher who sometimes stopped his sermon to say you still with us Sister Phoenicia. Law me, she said, what have I gone and done. I be thinkin' that I gots to tell someone lest Baby come back after I pass and be accused of takin' a life, and it plum slip my mind that Samuel Daniel gonna be in dangerous trouble if they find out he help us out like he did.

It slipped her mind until she had already told about how he came along, waded into the water, rescued them, took them home, told them he'd bury Oliver Ray's body, took the shovel, walked to the field, unhitched the mule and give him a gentle whack to send him home, dragged Oliver Ray Spears' body like it was a dead limb off a tree.

Samuel Daniel McElroy had thought to load the body onto his wagon, cover it with barrel head-ings, drive through Sugars Spring and bury him deep in the soft soil between Yellow Creek and Hominy. He would have too if he hadn't realized he was about to be come upon by bird hunters heading home to escape the torrent that was surely coming. Instead, he dragged Oliver Ray Spears' dead weight to the thicket that edged the field where Rebekah

Sarah and Phoenicia had left him and stuffed him in a hollow log. He packed both ends of the log with black dirt, the same black dirt that, all those years later, Tump Dyer and Bobo Hughes dug out so they could crawl through, pretending to be escaping from Indians and Germans led by Geronimo and Kaiser somebody.

It slipped Phoenicia's mind until nearing the end of the story and then she jumped as if startled by the quick movement of something like a mouse running under her feet, or a martin darting close to the porch. She said oh lawd, whatever possessed me to give out Samuel Daniel's name like I just done. She said I 'low if this gets him into trouble Beelzebub's gonna claim my soul. And as the locust started buzzing with the setting sun, Phoenicia said lawdy she hoped all those years of giving preachers jars of her pickled peaches, green tomato preserves and muscadine jelly, and a few other good deeds she'd tried to do like visiting shut-ins and such, would balance out that one awful mark and maybe, just maybe, God Almighty would just tear up that page and throw it away.

Cora Emery, in all her honesty, neglected to tell David Ben Sugars some of what she had seen that day—only telling what she had not. She had *not* seen any other cars or trucks go by—how could she since she was at David Ben Sugars' house baking pies with his wife, Little Jewel. And that much was true. Cora Emery got home from her day of pie baking in time to see Phoenicia and Rebekah Sarah trudging back home across the fields of Johnson grass, leaving their old mule Cornelius behind them, looking like he was hitched even though they hadn't used their mule in years. They were at such a distance and with the darkening sky as a backdrop, she had to recognize them by their shapes—one like Humpty Dumpty and the other like a stick figure—heading toward their house. Cora Emery started across the field to them to see what they might be doing and if they needed help when suddenly a voice inside her head said *leave it be*.

Truth be told, it wasn't just inside her head. She heard the voice as if it were carried in the wind that was now floating through the still, hot day. It was a woman's voice, one that she knew she had heard at one time in her life but couldn't place. *Leave it be* the voice said again. It was warm, the voice, this woman's voice. Warm, soft as down, but not to be disobeyed. Cora Emery looked at the cloud that had gathered so quickly, shook her head and said aloud Cora Emery you been hangin' around Rebekah Sarah far too much. Then she shook her head again to make sure her hearing was back to normal. And she turned back toward home.

Cora Emery never mentioned that to anyone, or that after getting her tea towels off the line she had seen Samuel Daniel McElroy right before the coming of rain, had seen his tall, wide-shouldered silhouette as the skies opened up, the voice once again telling her to let it be.

One day in 1950, a letter came to the post office, addressed "To the nearest relation to Rebekah Sarah Weaver or Fanicia Standfry" saying Jasmine Rose, their granddaughter, had died an untimely death and had requested before she died to be buried beside her grandmamas. Miz Lular Bell, the postmistress, made it a practice to give letters addressed to dead people and letters that took figuring out what they meant to the county sheriff. Little Jewel Sugars took care of such letters for her husband, so it was she who arranged for Jasmine Rose to be buried next to Phoenicia—without fanfare since the letter said there had been a proper funeral service in St. Louis—and only Little Jewel, Cora Emery, Montgomery Sugars, Samuel Daniel McElroy, two of his daughters and a handful of members of the Bethel Baptist Tabernacle Church attended the burial.

The person who wrote the letter also sent considerably more money than it took to bring Baby back and bury her, so Little Jewel Sugars, feeling obliged to use every penny for the cause it was intended, bought a huge pink granite gravestone.

There it sits in Bethel Cemetery—which the whites call Chickenham Graveyard—among the tin markers and the few skinny white limestone ones that are mostly fallen over and cracked. The gravestone says simply *Jasmine Rose*.

Young folks who don't listen to porch tales, or folks who are new to the towns, or folks who wander the countryside taking rubbings from weathered markers wonder about the pink granite gravestone, they wonder about Jasmine Rose, they wonder why she doesn't have a last name, or if Rose is her last name, or what year she was born, and died. They wonder if she ever married, or had children. They look at that gigantic gravestone, pink as an April sunset, and wonder who it was that loved her.

5

The Choosing of
Little Jewel

*Who can find a virtuous woman? For her
price is far above rubies.*

Proverbs 31:10

1924

When David Ben Sugars and Little Jewel Flowers, who at sixteen years of age was eight years his junior, eloped on the fourteenth of February, everyone in Sugars Spring opened their mouths in disbelief at the match between sweet but plain Little Jewel, who had been raised in the strictest of Christian families, who until that day had never defied her parents in any way, and the divinely handsome David Ben, who having been raised by slipped-away Methodists did not even profess to be a Christian. True, David Ben had also never defied his parents but that was because his mother who ruled the roost in the Sugars' household had never given him any rules to defy.

Folks at Pleasant Gilbert's store shook their heads and said they'd never have dreamed David Ben would have chosen Little Jewel—who they had fully expected would marry Cecil Coop the young song leader at the Baptist church. They said Little Jewel would rue the day she had succumbed to David Ben even though they could understand how someone so handsome and with such a pleasing disposition could draw her into his spell. They said he was spoiled rotten since the day he came into this world so he wouldn't have any idea how to take care of a family.

They said his four sisters—as pretty as they were—had worked sunup to sundown since they were knee high to toadstools but that David Ben had been given free rein to do just what he wanted. If he wanted to quit his chores in the middle of the day, go sit under their catawba tree and read some book, Montgomery brought him lemonade before she went back to mending fences, plowing, or herding livestock up from the bottomland. They said David Ben—except for splittin' wood—spent his days reading or playing baseball, spent his nights carousing with war buddies from Hope, or just carousing.

They said what else would you expect. They said Montgomery had robbed the cradle when she'd married J. D. Sugars, her being eighteen and him being only fifteen. They said she was in the family way at the time or else why would a Sugars marry a

Sutton since the whole lot of them, the Suttons, had left Alabama in the middle of the night, in 1880, when Montgomery was a tiny child, bringing everything they had in broken-down wagons pulled by broken-down oxen. They said that sounded mighty suspicious to them.

They said Montgomery babied her husband like he was still in diapers or like he had slaves to wait on him the way his daddy and granddaddy's had, so of course she would baby the baby of the family. They said J.D. used to sit under a shade tree on a hot day watching Montgomery and their mule break ground, hollering now Montgomery don't let yourself get sunstroke.

They said she sure was partial to men. They said when she was carrying David Ben after having given birth to four daughters she had been heard to say if that baby turned out to be another goldang split-tail she was going to give her to the gypsies the next time they camped out in their pasture.

They said after David Ben came back from the war, Montgomery—being so elated that he came back intact—had worsened her indulgence. They said she made J.D. drive her to Hope, extract some of their savings from the bank and buy David Ben an automobile when they didn't yet own anything but an old truck that had been abused by its first owner.

They said Montgomery was milking her old Jersey when she got word of the elopement from the mail carrier. They said she said words like goldang and worse and in her exasperation kicked over the bucket which was at least two-thirds full of milk making her swear even more saying words too bad to mention.

They said again and again that Montgomery Sugars had made it impossible for David Ben to be a husband of any worth. They said yessirree David Ben and Little Jewel will be spending their whole lives living with Montgomery making the two daughters still living at home wait on him. They said meek Little Jewel will fade into the background like a tiny bud on flowered wallpaper, they said she will fold up like beeblossom when it's touched. They said Little Jewel will be eaten up by the women of the Sugars' household just like the quails go after beeblossom seed. They said after a while, no one will notice she's there.

After five weeks of living with the Sugars women, Little Jewel, who—as far as anyone knew—had never given an order in her life, took David Ben out to the smoke shed for privacy and said it simply was not right for his parents to take care of them, that it was their responsibility to provide for themselves. She told David Ben he had to find a job and support them or she would go back to her father's house.

To everyone's surprise, David Ben did just that,

went to work for the heading company, found a tiny house on the outskirts of Sugars Spring for him and his wife, and later for their daughter, Virginia Alexandria. Montgomery was vexed at Little Jewel for giving birth to a split-tail, vexed to the point that she didn't even go see the baby. But Little Jewel on her first outing had bundled her baby and taken it to Montgomery, had walked down into the pasture where Montgomery was pulling up bitterweed and said isn't she beautiful Miz Montgomery to which Montgomery replied how can anything with three chins be beautiful.

Little Jewel somehow managed to laugh when Montgomery said it, and laughed about it later when she told it at Pleasant Gilbert's even though the folks at the store knew it must have broken her heart.

They said Little Jewel will be a saint if she can keep that up, if she can endure such a mother-in-law. They said Montgomery will be a thorn in Little Jewel's side until the day she dies.

Her husband is known in the gates when he sitteth among the elders in the land.
Proverbs 31:23

1929

One rainy Saturday in May, David Ben—losing touch with his gentle disposition—took on three of his uncles (Montgomery's brothers) who were as big and rawboned as his mother was small-boned and tiny. The fight began on the porch of Pleasant Gilbert's store when one of the uncles made a remark disparaging David Ben's war-widowed sister with lavender eyes. J.D.'s nephew jumped in on David Ben's side to help the odds. Soon other cousins, neighbors and even Horace Higginbottom, the school principal—who sided with the uncles as to the characterization of the war-widowed sister—joined in the mayhem which spilled out onto the road like tumbleweed, spilled into Tucker Martin's front yard, and ended when David Ben, being restrained by two uncles, shook his arms loose and hit the third uncle on the head with a tire iron.

The cut would have seemed even worse if the third uncle had not been wearing a spanking-new felt hat which to everyone's bafflement had remained on his head throughout the foray, a felt hat which acted as a blotter, absorbing much of the blood. David Ben would have gone to prison since the third uncle who hadn't spoken to Montgomery for ten years filed charges, causing Montgomery to throw a conniption to match all her others and threaten any judge who tried to put her son in jail with a kick in the seat of his pants or better yet in the front of his pants.

At Montgomery's request, J. D. Sugars' brother—a well-respected man who had been the recipient of the get-up-and-go in the family and who worked for the highway commission, giving him contacts at the state house—intervened, and David Ben was given a choice: he could spend time in prison, or he could accept a commission as deputy sheriff and help clean up Hampstead County which in the bad times of the nation was rife with moonshine, family disputes, theft and various acts of vagrancy.

Folks felt sorry for the mess Little Jewel Flowers found herself in. They said being such a fine Christian woman, she would of course bear her suffering in silence even though she must be thoroughly ashamed to show her face. So they scratched their heads the next Friday when Little Jewel, waiting to see the newest pattern on the flour sacks Pleasant was unloading, announced that the choice was strictly up to her husband, but that she knew—in her heart of hearts—her husband would make a fine sheriff so maybe the fight had been a thing of providence.

Montgomery, whose family had hauled all their possessions from Alabama in one covered wagon when she was four and whose grandpa, it was rumored, had fought on the side of the Union, told her son if he put on that badge she'd better never hear he went around mistreatin' niggers and poor folks just because he could.

So David Ben became a deputy, keeping his job at the heading company—since deputying paid only pennies and especially since he had two more mouths to feed when Little Jewel gave birth to twins named Rose and Sharon, whose arrival caused Montgomery to throw her face toward the sky and say what have I done to deserve all these split-tails, all these two-legged creatures. And when Montgomery's war-widowed daughter repeated that to Little Jewel, Little Jewel laughed so hard she literally did split a stitch.

Within a few years everyone came to know that David Ben was born to sheriffing the way someone might be born to be a ballplayer or a ballerina or president or to no good. He could sniff out stills better than a black-and-tan could catch the scent of a deer. He could usually calm down drunks and talk them into going home and sleeping it off. And if necessary he could wrestle down a man twice his size.

When he caught ten-year-old Thurman Eugene Myers, the leader of the mischief makers, putting glue on the rockers at Birdwell's Boarding House he placed his large hands gently on Thurman Eugene's shoulders and in a voice heavy with sadness said son I'm gonna have to take you to jail for a *long, long time* so you go home and tell your mama good-bye and get yourself packed and I'll be along d'reckly.

Thurman Eugene spent the day under his bed before getting the word from his mother that Deputy Sugars in a spirit of good-heartedness had decided to give him one more chance. After that, mischievous pranks diminished considerably.

Folks at Pleasant Gilbert's store shook their heads and said who would have dreamed that David Ben Sugars had the wisdom of Solomon.

Can a man take fire in his bosom, and his clothes not be burned?

Proverbs 6:27

1934–1935

In June of '34, five years after becoming deputy, David Ben Sugars was elected county sheriff and would be sworn in on the first of January, but the next month the reigning sheriff had to step down due to ailing health, so David Ben assumed his duties in July, giving him the wherewithal to leave his foreman job and be a full-time sheriff, and giving his family a secure albeit modest means of riding out the hard times.

The fall of that year he was occupied with trying to solve the murder of Oliver Ray Spears, the constable of the township. And even though he was unable to do so, he kept the confidence of the people by the otherwise fine accomplishments of his first year as sheriff—chief among them was busting up four stills, busting up the rustling ring, and busting the jaw of a drunk who had wrecked the 1935 Juneteen Celebration in Bethel.

In the fall of '35, he was summoned on an urgent matter to the outskirts of Hope where a man had gone berserk and beat his wife so that one side of her face swelled up double, one eye was fast on the way to gluing shut, and blood caked the edges of her red hair, which—David Ben noticed even in the heat of the dispute—was almost as red as Isannah Sanders' who had left Sugars Spring shortly after the cyclone of 1920. A cyclone which left Isannah hanging by her long hair in a black oak, hair so red it threatened to burst into flame, and which left David Ben Sugars about to burst into flame when he saw her sitting on the ground all wet and safe and see-through in her drenched white gown.

David Ben gave the woman's husband a hand-chop under his chin, knocking him unconscious, and hauled him to jail. When the husband came to, David Ben told him if he ever again laid a hand on his wife, or any woman for that matter, he would kill him. A few weeks later, the husband went berserk again, standing in the road, blocking traffic, yelling obscene things and threatening to kill his wife who stood in their doorway with a shotgun, forbidding him entrance.

A neighbor had run like a chased rabbit a mile to the nearest phone, but the call didn't reach the sheriff quickly enough this time, and when the husband, axe drawn back in his hand, lunged at the woman, she shot him.

David Ben called the coroner, took testimony from a couple who had been witnesses as they sat in their car waiting for the husband to get out of the road, took testimony from the scattered neighbors on that road. Then he asked some of the women to look after the wife whose scarlet hair conspired to magnify her paleness making her skin milk white, making her seem drained of her last drop of blood, her last spark of life.

David Ben Sugars agonized that he didn't get there in time to prevent her from undergoing such an ordeal, even if he had been compelled to kill the man himself—something he had yet been spared the duty of doing, even in his brief touch with war.

David Ben Sugars agonized over the scab crusting the side of her face. David Ben Sugars agonized over the look in the woman's eyes, eyes the color of silver, or a rain cloud. David Ben Sugars agonized over the sheer beauty of her porcelain skin.

He agonized for a fortnight. One evening at dusk, he finished his work at his courthouse office and left Hope heading for home. But when he came to the road that turned to Sugars Spring he passed on by and found himself driving down the back road, the road he had told himself he would not take. He slowed down to a crawl and drove by her house, looking at the soft lights in her front rooms, looking at the clouds, clouds full of thunderheads coming from the south, clouds that would soon make the sky midnight dark.

He drove on by, relieved that he hadn't

stopped, telling himself he had no intention of stopping, telling himself he should get home before the cloud caught up with him making his drive home in poor vision over rain-swept roads hazardous. Maybe the coming rain would dampen the burning—like hot coals—inside him.

But wasn't it his duty, his obligation as sheriff to offer assistance to one who had suffered through such an ordeal? This road, he knew, was a dead end. He had to go back by her house anyway, to get back on the road to home, so he pulled his Ford in at the next pasture gate, backed out and headed back, telling himself he would simply find out if she was mending. He looked south and saw the clouds dark as indigo. No doubt about that sky. A storm was coming.

Passing through the street near her corner;
and he went the way to her house.

Proverbs 7:8

David Ben Sugars walked up to the woman's front porch, drawn to the light like a June bug. When he reached her front door and saw through the circle of glass—glass covered only by thin lace curtains—that there was no one in the living room, he felt a certain sense of relief, of escape. Of salvation even.

But she had seen him, had seen him when he

drove by the first time and she had put her hand to her chest and said please dear God make him stop, so as David Ben turned to go a voice as soft as cotton floated out the small opening in the window, a voice with the welcome formality of a church greeter, saying please come in.

David Ben Sugars stepped inside with the reverence of one entering the waiting room at a funeral parlor. He felt her eyes upon him first. Then he turned and saw her in the next room, sitting at her vanity in a dressing gown so pale green it was almost white, bathing in the warm colors thrown by a stained glass lamp, brushing her hair with a silver brush.

She stood up slowly, then reached down and turned out the lamp. She stood there in the dark, lifted the brush, let it glide down her hair one more time, strands flying away from the brush breaking into sparks like fireflies.

She stepped into the living room and looked him in the eye, feeling no need to smile, unlike most women he knew in greeting a guest. He saw a flash like lightning in her gray eyes, eyes the color of thunderclouds.

He turned his eyes to keep her hair from burning them, he turned his eyes to keep her eyes from striking, his eyes taking refuge in the painted lamp in the living room, the lamp that was throwing colors on the floor, on the wall, a lamp with green vines and purple flowers.

He looked at the vine wrapping itself around the lamp, tangling itself in the flowers. He said I just wanted to check on you, to see how you're doing. She said I have some coffee left over from supper I can heat it up.

She served it to him in her living room, offered it to him in a cup of fine china which caused his bronzed hands trying to figure out how to hold the paper-thin cup to seem even larger then they were, caused his hands to seem so gentle the thought of them touching her face or her shoulders brought a flush to her pale skin, brought color to her lips so that he saw them turn red right before his eyes, the rich red of raspberries.

David Ben Sugars put the cup down with urgency, splashing the stale coffee onto the cutwork doily on her serving table, and said I should be getting home. She stood up and said nothing.

He heard the first thunder of the cloud that had lurked behind him when he left the courthouse. He felt himself falling into the storm. He tried to shift his weight toward the foot nearest the door. He said my wife will have supper waiting.

She said I understand. But she did not release him with those eyes. The cloud was upon them now, and the lightning that had flashed in the distance turned to streaks like flailing tentacles over the town of Hope, coming closer to the house of the woman who two weeks ago to the day shot and killed her husband, and who now stood tall and silent before a peace officer as if waiting to be judged, who stood looking into his brown eyes, eyes edged with gold to match his golden skin, eyes that tore themselves from her to gaze at the delicate porcelain china cups, to gaze at the many-colored lamp, to gaze at the flame in the gas-burning stove before surrendering and traveling up her dressing gown, so pale green it was almost white, like the blossom of honeylocust, and looking into the fire and smoke of her eyes.

Then they both knew he could travel no further even though he said once more with what he hoped, even maybe prayed was conviction, I'm late enough as it is.

She said please be careful, she said it's getting so dark out, she said it will be hard to see in the downpour that's surely coming.

As she said the word, rain fell from the cloud, hitting the tin roof drop by drop at first and then issuing forth in a rhythm like parade drums.

He said she always keeps my supper warm. She said your wife is the most fortunate woman on this earth.

The rain no longer had any rhythm, pounding the tin roof of the house on the outskirts of Hope with such fierceness no one inside could have heard any more words even if they had shouted them.

A jagged claw of lightning accompanied by a piercing sound struck the front-yard elm slicing a huge limb which broke into flame before being smothered by the blanket of rain. But David Ben Sugars and the woman with hair as crimson as the sunrise outside his window when he woke up that morning didn't even notice.

She looketh well to the ways of her household, and eateth not the bread of idleness.

Proverbs 31:27

David Ben Sugars drove up to his house in the light of a pear-colored morning just as Little Jewel was preparing breakfast. Even before he got out of the car, something nipped at her that this time he has not been watching a still, this time he has not been hiding in a pasture waiting for cattle rustlers, this time he has not been on a robbery stakeout based on tips he'd received.

Because the morning sun was behind him, she could see only his silhouette in the doorway. She struck a match to light a burner on their kitchen stove, the match flaming yellow, then golden. She watched the flame ease down the match. She watched the flame, blue at its origin but burning gold. She watched the charred wood turn black then flare crimson then black again, the flare of crimson almost too brief to be seen. She knew her husband had been with another woman.

And even though he had hardly mentioned her, Little Jewel knew it was the woman who had killed her husband. That knowledge pounded into her head with such force that she went into the bathroom and threw up. Then she washed her face, went back into the kitchen and set the skillet for the eggs onto the burner.

David Ben picked at his breakfast, went to bed and feigned sleep for a few hours. Then he drove to Fulton to see an old man who said vagrants had been stealing jars of pickled peaches from his root cellar even though it beat all why they hadn't touched a single jar of anything else and why they hadn't taken any of the greens or one single squash from his garden.

Then David Ben drove to the courthouse. This time he was home in time for supper with an embroidered handkerchief from Briant's Drug Store in Hope as an offering for Little Jewel. Little Jewel said you don't need to buy me fancy things. He said I want to be good to you always.

At supper he and Little Jewel and the girls sat around the table and Little Jewel said girls, after supper you have to sing your new song for Daddy. Then when Little Jewel had tucked the girls in bed, had listened to their prayers, had told them to have sweet dreams, she and her husband bundled up against the cold and sat on the porch, hearing the sound of a distant radio, watching the dusty light of early evening give way to dark, watching lights in the rooms of nearby houses come on. Or go off.

Little Jewel said you have to promise to give

her up, the woman who shot her husband, or I'm taking the girls and leaving.

They sat in silence until the air hanging between them seemed to moan of its own heaviness, still he could not bring himself to give the answer they both wanted. He said I should be the one to leave. She said I could not bear to sleep in this house just now. He said where will you go, to your sisters, to your parents, where? And she said I will move in with Miz Cora Emery for the time being.

Miz Cora Emery's a good woman he said.

When Little Jewel Flowers packed her clothes and her daughters' clothes in sacks and moved in with Cora Emery McRae, the Yankee woman who had lived her adult life in Sugars Spring, who had been married and widowed there, folks scratched their heads in a state of dismay and disbelief—not so much that David Ben might from time to time succumb to the arms of another woman since with his manly looks, and with his station in life, women were sure to throw themselves at him—instead they were shocked that Little Jewel had not had the patience to turn a blind eye to it, to wait it out the way a woman who wanted to keep her man—at this stage in his life—would do.

They said they would never have suspected Little Jewel Sugars would leave her husband no matter what he did—for the sake of her children, they said.

They said David Ben was without question a good father. They said David Ben was such a fine sheriff, and before that a fine provider, and he had even taken Jesus into his life the first Sunday after his twin daughters were born.

Then they went back further and remembered how the women had set snares for him when he was first home from the war, how he could have had his choice of any woman in the county, how he never seemed to settle on one for very long, how they would have never dreamed he would marry someone who, though a good woman, was quite ordinary in appearance.

They remembered how they had thought he would get snared by May Ellen Huntley, their old Methodist minister's daughter and a loose young woman of the town. They remembered how they had been certain something would come of David Ben and the beautiful Isannah Sanders after her husband, the Baptist minister, was killed in the cyclone of 1920—and maybe it would have too if Isannah, still in a state of shock over her dear husband's death, hadn't up and moved a short time later without telling hardly anyone she was leaving.

Some of them actually had thought something would've come of David Ben and Isannah *before* her husband's death if David Ben had any choice in the matter because they had seen how he looked at her, and they remembered how the vision of Isannah Sanders—Isannah with eyes as gray as smoke

and hair as red as Cupid's heart—lingered after
Isannah herself had long passed through a place,
lingered like the scent of jasmine, lingered like fog.

They remembered what an affirmation it was
that Isannah had been such an upright Christian
woman, as upright as Little Jewel herself. But Isannah had been much more comely. And they wondered if David Ben and Little Jewel had simply been
mismatched where outward beauty was concerned.

Olivia Duckett made the mistake of wondering
aloud at young Doc Walker's office as Cora Emery
McRae was picking up some paregoric for one of
Little Jewel's daughters. Olivia's exact words were I
always did wonder how someone as plain as Little
Jewel Flowers reined in someone like David Ben.
Cora Emery's exact words were well Olivia if it
takes beauty to get a fine-looking man, that ex-
plains why your husband was so ugly he'd scare the
feathers off a duck.

Later Cora Emery felt a bit bad since Eldon
Duckett had been a friend of her James. And a nice
man at that. But she figured Eldon was dead so he
wouldn't suffer any from her remarks.

After Cora Emery had left, after Olivia Duckett
had been administered a whiff of spirits of ammo-
nia, the waiting customers and patients at young
Doc Walker's said it was a shame because David
Ben Sugars was such a fine sheriff, they said they
didn't suppose he had a ghost's chance of getting
elected again when election time rolled around, they

said what's gotten into Cora Emery, they said no one wants a sheriff who can't keep a wife. They said if Little Jewel didn't wake up she was going to turn their lives into shambles.

They sighed and said ultimately the blame had to be placed on Montgomery Sugars who had raised him to think the world was his for the taking.

Montgomery Sugars paid a call to her daughter-in-law the minute the news reached her farm. The visit was brief because the two women had never shared the same language. Montgomery said I only got a minute but I wanted to tell you I'll damn sure see to it that you and Cora Emery here and the girls get all the meat y'all need, y'all sure as hell won't go hungry as long as I have a cow in my pasture and goddamn breath in this body. And Little Jewel said God bless you Miz Montgomery and I'll be sure and bring the girls to see you when I can.

David Ben Sugars was hardly seen in Sugars Spring. He took his meals in Hope at the City Cafe, or at the Unique Sandwich Shop or even at the jail. The first week he slept on a cot at the jail trying to remember all the things he loved about Little Jewel which were many.

He had first been attracted to her when he was twenty and home from the war. Little Jewel was only twelve at the time and he was drawn not in a passionate way but in a way he couldn't describe.

He knew it made him happy to see her skipping by on the way to school. Her friends walking with her tried valiantly to walk like ladies especially, he knew, when they saw him in his yard. But Little Jewel would see him and start skipping like the very sight of him made her so happy she couldn't walk if she tried. He knew of course that she was sweet on him as were many other young girls, and older women, so he did nothing to encourage her. And he spent the next few years in the company of many women, mostly for a short time and mostly for a walk, or holding hands or kissing.

Then came the time of May Ellen Huntley the daughter of the minister who was renowned for inviting men to slip through her bedroom window. The first night that he had kissed her, had run his hands up and down her grass green dress was the night of a baseball game, and he had picked her up in his car, and they had driven to one of the swamp landings. He had kissed her and run his hands across her pearly shoulders until he thought he was drowning in a sea of green. That he remembered.

And the first night he had the courage to lift the screen she had left unlatched for him, even though her daddy, the minister, was sleeping down the hall, she let him lie on top of her, both of them staying fully clothed, let him grind his groin against her until they knew he was going to explode. She said it's time for you to leave now, go in the bushes and take care of yourself before you get home or you'll be in pain for sure. He wondered if a woman needed the same kind of relief.

One late summer night, a night with the hint of fall in the air, he lay on top of May Ellen the way he always did. Then she said let me show you something else. She lifted her skirt, her petticoats. Underneath was a pair of pink pants, shiny, full like a skirt, only very short. Smiling, she took his hand and guided it inside her pants, guided it to a mound of hair. Then she sat up, holding his hand there, and—using her other hand—unbuttoned his trousers, her smile frozen on her face, her eyes as blue as an ice block staring into his. He had to look away. He knew he must be as hard as iron and it only took a few strokes and he shot hot liquid out, some of it flying through the air, some of it running over her hands. She took a handkerchief and wiped her hands and then gave it to him to wipe himself. It would be more enjoyable if I let you put that inside me she said but I don't want a bastard child. If you want me, you've got to marry me, and she smiled yet again.

He came to realize he felt nothing for May Ellen Huntley except a certain respect at her sense of freedom and defiance, and except for the feeling a dog must get for a bitch in heat.

He began avoiding her even though she seemed to lie in wait for him behind every tree in the village, flashing her precise smile and her ice blue eyes. Finally, though, she took up with Floyd Dillard who broke wedding plans with another girl and asked May Ellen to marry him. She said yes, and then ran off a few weeks later with a Watkins salesman.

Up until the time David Ben married Little Jewel, that had been the extent of his experience in exploring a woman's body and the needs of his own.

He had heard white men talking about visiting colored women, and he had felt drawn to Delie Turner, when he watched her walk by the Sugars place on her way to town. He had heard that William Burl Cane spent nights with her, and he envied him. And he dreamed of her one whole spring. He once dreamed that he was getting into bed with her and her arms, brown and smooth, were stretched out to him, and he was about to touch her thick hair, wavy and glistening, when his sister woke him up by throwing a dipper of water in his face, saying I don't care if Mama did say to let you sleep, get outa bed so I can wash those sheets.

After Delie was blown away in the storm, his dreams stopped.

He had dreamed, both waking and sleeping, about Isannah Sanders, even before the tornado left her husband with a board pierced through his head, and left Isannah hanging by her long red hair, hanging high in the black oak. He had been the one to bring her down the ladder, thrown over his shoulder like a sack of flour. The feeling of her warm wet body against him had been the most exciting feeling he had known. He knew, then, that he loved this woman whose hair had saved her life. And in his dreams when he lay beside her and kissed her, her long hair slowly wrapped around him, entangling him like honeysuckle vines around a lamp post.

But that had happened only in a young man's dreams. Early one morning, when he finally called on Isannah Sanders—at the old Cantrell place, the deserted house she moved into after the storm— called on her on his way home from a night of playing cards with his army buddies from Hope, their talk about women giving him the boldness to approach her house in the pink light of dawn with an offer to split her wood, his dreams had come to an abrupt ending.

He had knocked softly and no one had answered. Armed with the courage from a night of cards with men who wove more tales than he could imagine, he walked around to the back of her house to see if she was in the kitchen.

And that's when he saw them through a slit in her back bedroom curtains, saw, or thought he saw, Isannah's hair tangled around a body, too dark to be a white man, and he knew instantly she had taken Samuel Daniel McElroy into her bed. He stepped back in such shock that he knocked over a rake that was leaning against the house. Then he took off running, hoping they hadn't heard him, hoping they wouldn't see him, hoping he had not seen what he thought he'd seen.

Isannah Sanders left town that week. Took her son William and moved, he heard, to Memphis but he never knew for sure. They said she just couldn't stand living in Sugars Spring with such strong memories of her husband. David Ben never told anyone, never even gave Samuel Daniel who was—as much as could be—a friend, never gave him a hint of what he had seen.

The rage he might have felt was tempered by his awe that Isannah Sanders and Samuel Daniel McElroy would have the audacity to consummate the lust that burned inside them. He thanked the powers that be that it had not been Floyd Dillard or any of a hundred other men in town that had witnessed such a sight as he had witnessed.

That was before he came to his senses and realized it was his imagination, that it was the way the shadows fell, and his tired eyes from being up all night, and all the talk that his card-playing friends were given to, that what he saw had been a colored man at all. It was the shadows that made him look so dark, that made it look like anyone at all. After all Isannah Sanders, everyone knew, was beyond reproach.

One day, four years later, the day Little Jewel Flowers turned sixteen, their paths met and he walked her to school. This time she did not skip, but he thought she was fighting hard not to. By the time they got to the lane that led to the school, he knew that he wanted to marry this girl with the flyaway hair, round face and slightly overlapping teeth, this girl with eyes the color of a robin's eggs, this girl who seemed to lap at life the way a hungry kitten laps at a bowl of milk.

The first week, sleeping at the jail, David Ben remembered walking Little Jewel to school and he remembered how happy he'd been. Then he remembered the woman's full red mouth on his, and her skin like white silk. He remembered the blue veins trailing down her neck, a neck splashed with a perfume he could not name, a neck so smooth he wanted to put his mouth to it, his teeth to it, to devour her.

By the end of that week all he could think about was the spicy fragrance of her sheets, and he knew he had to put his face against those sheets one more time even if they smothered him.

This time it was late and her house was in total darkness, but he didn't consider not stopping, he didn't consider not knocking. He would knock until he waked the dead if need be.

Her door flew open at the first knock and soon he was melting into her body, and soon he was in her bed, smelling the spices in her rose bowl, on her sheets, on her neck, making him believe he could jump off a water tower and soar, he could pick her up and hold her above his head as an offering to the gods, he could lift the world, hold it above him, like Atlas in the stories he had read when he was a boy, making him believe he could send the world and everyone in it hurling into the dark and boundless space beyond the stars.

David Ben Sugars didn't return to his bed in his office at the jail, spending his nights instead in the down and feather bed of this woman, his body tangled—like molten bronze—in her flaming hair. And when they lay there having fed their certain hunger, when she felt pins sticking his heart she said I would never ask you to leave her but I beg you never to leave me, she said you can come to me anytime night or day, she said I have to have you or I will simply fade away into thin air, into nothingness.

Then she'd place her full lips to his ear, and slide soft kisses down his cheek, down his neck, she'd roll her tongue on his nipples, she'd slide down, down, doing things he had only dreamed about a woman doing, dreamed about Delie Turner doing, or May Ellen Huntley doing, and mostly dreamed about Isannah Sanders doing those things, things he didn't know a woman would really want to do.

He rolled her over on her back, put his mouth to her breast swollen and waiting for him, and sucked one and then the other, gently at first but harder as he felt her nipples harden, her body arching, her legs reaching around him, locking him to her as she said come inside me, come inside me, her voice rising until she'd scream oh please pour yourself into me. And he would.

It wasn't until he had tasted every part of her that he knew her first name, and sometimes he called her name when she laid on top of him, riding him like he was a wild bronco. But later, as he lay by her sleeping body, lay there in the dark, it was another name that ran through his mind, fueling the fire burning inside him, the fire that, he knew, would eventually consume him.

Still, he lay there with her crimson hair spreading across his chest like small red rivers, knowing he would travel each tributary even if he got lost and never found his way out.

In the light of day, he missed Little Jewel who had made him believe he could keep his feet firmly planted in this world, and that he had an important place in it. And he missed his daughters. And Sugars Spring.

By Thanksgiving Day, the hunger for his wife and family had become an ache, so he drove up as Cora Emery was deviling eggs and Little Jewel was preparing a pecan pie. After Rose and Sharon sat on his lap and clung to his arms and said when are you coming to take us home Daddy, after nine-year-old Virginia announced she wanted to be called Ginger from now on and that she loved living with Miz Cora Emery and hoped they stayed there forever, after Cora Emery said you can stay for dinner if you want since it's Thanksgiving, and Little Jewel said no I don't think that's a good idea, and after Little Jewel said girls go with Miz Cora Emery to feed her new baby chickens, David Ben and Little Jewel sat

across from each other in the living room, the smells
of a Thanksgiving feast drifting from the kitchen.

David Ben looked at Little Jewel, her short
dark hair darting in all directions, he looked out the
window at Cora Emery McRae and his daughters
and meant it when he said I love you and I want to
come home.

Little Jewel said does this mean you will give
up the woman who shot her husband. Silence again
stretched before them, silence unable to soak up
the agony darting about them, unable to muffle the
groaning in their hearts. He wanted to say yes, he
tried to say yes, and even though he might lie to
himself, he could not lie to this woman with eyes the
color of robins' eggs. All he could do was sit there
bearing the weight of his guilt, and desire—a weight
that caused his strong shoulders to sag.

He said I love you and I want us to go home.
He said I'll be good to you.

And Little Jewel Sugars—feeling a pain so
strong she almost had to put her hand to her heart
but would not let herself—drew what she felt like
would be her last breath and said I'll be talking to a
lawyer tomorrow.

But that evening, Rose and Sharon and Virginia
came down with stomachaches which kept Little
Jewel up most of the night, so she postponed the visit
to the lawyer one more day. Early the afternoon of
the day after Thanksgiving, when the girls were
sleeping, albeit fitfully, and Cora Emery and Little
Jewel, having finished the dinner dishes, sat at the

kitchen table looking over the latest Montgomery Ward's catalog, they saw his car coming down the road, coming so slow the red dirt barely lifted behind the wheels, lifted only enough to make a pink haze just above ground level before settling down from whence it came. David Ben knocked, taking off his Stetson as Cora Emery opened the door, but not bothering with amenities, looked past Cora Emery, looked through the living room to the kitchen to find Little Jewel thumbing through the apparel section, barely looking up to acknowledge him.

He said Little Jewel we have to go for a drive. Little Jewel said the girls have been sick so I don't want to leave them. She said you can say what you have to say right here.

So in the presence of God and Cora Emery McRae, David Ben Sugars, twisting his Stetson with his large hands, promised Little Jewel Sugars if she would take him back he would honor their wedding vows for the rest of his life.

By nightfall the three daughters of Little Jewel and David Ben Sugars were sleeping sound in their own beds, dreaming about the Christmas tree their daddy would go into the woods and get the next day. Earlier, the oldest one had told him her name was Virginia again.

Later in the sanctity of their bed, Little Jewel reached out for her husband, welcoming him with a desire that was nothing like the inferno he had walked through, but which had its own small flame burning slow, steady, keeping him warm.

The wife shall be as a fruitful vine by the sides
of thine house; thy children like olive plants
round about thy table.

Psalms 128:3

1935–1960

On Christmas Day, Little Jewel told David Ben she was carrying his child. She had actually known it for some weeks now, and had planned to tell him over supper, but that was the night he hadn't come home. She had not wanted him to come back to her for the sake of a child, so she had never mentioned it to anyone. Cora Emery had assumed Little Jewel's bout with nausea was a case of nerves. They named the fourth one Emery Montgomery which did nothing to prevent Montgomery's dismay at yet another girl. Nor was she placated when four years later, in 1940, they named the fifth girl Isabelle—who would quickly be called Sugarbell—after Montgomery's mother.

Then Virginia Alexandria (who came to be called Ginger in her teens) lost her boyfriend on a Sunday morning at a faraway place called Pearl Harbor, lost dear sweet Raymond Gentry who had grown up on the Columbus road and had won Montgomery's heart at the same time he'd won Ginger's. So when Little Jewel announced, shortly after, that she and David Ben were going to have their sixth child, Montgomery said this damn sure better not be a boy, saying she'd lost a son-in-law in the first war and now Raymond who one day would've been a grandson-in-law, she said we don't need to be raising three-legged creatures to die off in some God-forsaken place.

David Ben was at Hope when the last one came, came so quickly Little Jewel barely had time to get from the garden to their daybed. Ginger who was sixteen fetched Cora Emery and sent word to the doctor and to Montgomery, but by the time the doctor got there, the baby had arrived. Little Jewel said I'm going to name this one after the father even though she is a girl. I'm going to name her Benny. The doctor wrote in a scrawly hand, Bennie, then he said and what's the other name. Little Jewel's sister said how about Louise, and Little Jewel said well maybe and Ginger said I know Mama she said let's name her that pretty name of the woman who left some of her red hair in that tree we used to climb, the one that got blown up there by that tornado. And Little Jewel said why that's a wonderful idea, Benny Isannah it is.

David Ben rushed home as soon as he got the message. He said don't you think Benny Ruth or Benny Lou sounds better, and Little Jewel laughed and said come on honey, as I remember you had quite a crush on Isannah when you were a boy— that is before I lured you with my fatal beauty. And then she smiled her crooked smile that had become a thing of beauty to her husband. And he smiled and said then have it your way.

Montgomery and her two live-at-home daughters were in Texarkana at a cattle auction so they got the message when they arrived home at dusk. By the time they were on the scene, the baby had been named and bathed and visited by half the town. Montgomery said the baby might be right perty if they'd just cover up her four chins. She also told Little Jewel it was about time she and David Ben found out what was causing all those dang kids and do somethin' about it.

Little Jewel Sugars, never forgetting the solemnity and joylessness in her strict childhood home, raised her children in a home filled with the sounds of piano, guitars and a banjo, with the sounds of a thousand songs, and especially with the sound of laughter. She filled their house with good food, good stories, and goodwill. And she always reminded her children that they were blessed to have such a fine sheriff and good and gentle man for a father.

She knew of course that there were no guarantees in life so she went to church holding her Bible like one armed for battle, and she prayed earnestly for God to give her children good health and the strength to pass through whatever trials came their way.

*A good name is better than precious ointment;
and the day of death than the day of one's
birth.*

                                    Ecclesiastes 7:1

1960

When David Ben Sugars died in Little Jewel's
arms of a heart attack at age sixty, died one August
night as they sat on the couch watching *The Babe
Ruth Story* on television, he had been the duly
elected sheriff of Hampstead County for twenty-six
years. Black and white, rich and poor paid homage,
showing up by the hundreds on a day that was
ninety-nine degrees. The old women of Sugars
Spring said thank goodness Montgomery had died
two years before or this would have killed her. Samuel Daniel McElroy told David Ben's war-widowed
sister that the only people to take joy in his death
would be the bootleggers and those who loved evil.
The young women of Sugars Spring said he was still
a fine-looking man. They all said he'd be hard to
replace as sheriff. They said his family sure hadn'
given him many gray hairs.

When the funeral sermon was over, people
filed past the casket as Little Jewel and daughters
and sons-in-law and her eight grandchildren sat on
the first two rows, and the congregation sang *Will
the Circle Be Unbroken.* After all four verses, there
were still people who had not a chance to view so
they sang *Abide with Me,* which Little Jewel had

chosen in case they needed a second song. And as the congregation sang *fast falls the eventide, the darkness deepens, Lord with me abide,* Little Jewel Flowers Sugars felt as if her heart literally might be tearing, and she knew at fifty-two years of age she was beginning the darkest journey of her life. But, as she told everyone, she took solace in knowing she had been the most fortunate woman on this earth.

> *Let the husband render unto the wife due be-*
> *nevolence: and likewise also the wife unto the*
> *husband.*
>   1 Corinthians 7:3

1972

The women in the Sugars family gathered in the living room of the old Sugars place where the two youngest daughters—the unmarried one, and the war-widowed one—still lived. Those two had finished their chores. Little Jewel and Montgomery's two oldest daughters, who still lived near Sugars Spring, had finished the baking so the five of them stood decorating the Christmas tree and waiting for the arrival of Little Jewel's six daughters—the only grandchildren Montgomery Sugars would have, four of them with husbands and children—coming in from places long and far.

The women talked about old times and retold a thousand stories, many of them about the antics of

Montgomery. The war-widowed daughter thinking it was a story that they all knew and never dreaming it was a story Little Jewel hadn't heard said Little Jewel when you left Brother for runnin' round with that redhead in Hope and Mama heard you were gettin' a lawyer she yanked Papa up from the couch and said you get down to Hope right this minute and tell that sorry son of yours if he ever hopes to darken our doors again he better give that redhead up this very night, that if he wants to be your son he'll come back and do right by Little Jewel and his kids.

The unmarried daughter with skin still the color of ivory laughed and said I can still see Mama pushing Papa out that door saying if you can't talk sense into that boy's head you might as well not bother to come back home yourself. She said can you imagine Papa who wouldn't say boo to a fly going down and telling his son that he would disown him, but he did. He told him exactly that, and Brother came home to you with his tail between his legs.

A fleck of lavender in the war-widowed daughter's eyes flashed and she said yes exactly where it ought to have been all along. And all the women of the Sugars family had themselves a laugh, Little Jewel laughing as hard as the rest of them, not letting on that this was the first time she had ever heard the story, not letting on that she had closed her eyes to the talk at the time and had not even known the woman had red hair. And she wondered if it could possibly have been as red as Isannah Sanders' had been.

The second to oldest daughter who still had only a trace of gray in her hair said I never knew until then what Mama thought about you, specially since you kept having girls, lawdy she threw a fit every time someone came and told her it was another girl—never mind that she had four herself before she had Brother—but when she heard you were going to see a lawyer she told Papa go tell that son of ours if he don't come to his senses, we'll have one more daughter and no son cause Little Jewel Flowers is worth ten of him.

The oldest daughter whose green eyes had once sparkled like frost on grass said I never could figure Mama making Papa be the one to do that since she was the one who would walk up to the devil and ask him for a light, but Mama said there were things she could do better like running the farm—she said Papa coming from a bunch of spoilt damn slave owners couldn't plow a straight row so she preferred to do it herself. But she said since Papa kept his head in a book so much he was better with words.

The war-widowed daughter with flecks of lavender still in her eyes said yes, then right after telling Papa he was better with words Mama told him the exact words to say.

When Benny, the sixth daughter of David Ben

and Little Jewel and the one who lived the farthest away, drove up after a long, long journey, she opened her car door and heard the sound from the four aunts and her mother rolling out of the house. She said to Emery Ann, her daughter, see I told you the first thing we'd hear would be laughter.

I am my beloved's, and his desire is toward me.

Song of Solomon 7:10

1974

Little Jewel Sugars always worked at their gravesites on their anniversary. On this Valentine's, on what would have been their fiftieth anniversary, she arrived at the cemetery early in the day with rake, spade and shovel and two young azalea bushes for his and Cora Emery's graves, azalea bushes she had dug at what was still called the Cora Emery place even though some McRae cousins now owned it. Little Jewel was hoping they'd get another cold snap after such a warm winter spell, a cold snap that would urge the azaleas to bloom their first spring in a new place. She would help the sisters with Montgomery's and J.D.'s graves when spring had come to stay.

The unusually mild day was not unlike the February morning fifty years ago when she had told her parents good-bye, books in hand, and headed off to school. David Ben had never even kissed her yet, had only held her hand. She had thought she would die if he didn't kiss her soon. She was sure she would swoon at the first touch of his lips so she hoped they weren't standing when it happened.

She loved the way he took joy in everything she said. He began urging her to elope after he'd walked her to school five times. She was far too petrified of her father, Clinton Flowers, a stern, unsmiling, albeit a religious and good man, to do such a thing so each time she'd put him off. She'd said Papa will skin you alive and sell your pelt to Jasper Knight. And he had burst into laughter and said I am going to marry you girl, you might as well do it now as later. Or she'd say but I'm a Christian and you're not and if I marry you I won't rest until you are safe in the arms of Jesus and he'd laugh and say well you just might be the one to keep me from descending to Hell.

One day he said don't come to our spot in the morning unless you're going to marry me before noon. When she left for school she told herself she didn't have the courage, that her father wouldn't even permit her to be in the company of this wild young heathen as her father called him, so how could she defy her father and take David Ben Sugars for a husband. But when she got to the bend and had to decide to take the road to school or the road to the wooded spot in Honeycutt's clearing, she didn't even think of her father, or of school.

He was waiting for her there and when she saw him it was all she could do not to break into a skip.

Little Jewel had just begun clearing the grave of last year's dead stems before she was too warm. She took off her cardigan and placed it on his tombstone, a tombstone that said *As a Man thinketh in his heart, so is he.* Then she picked up the spade and began to break the soil in front of the tombstone where she would put the azaleas. If she put them any other place, Buster Thurman, the caretaker, would just mow them down, she'd learned that.

She'd learned right away that her new husband did indeed have a gentle soul and she had no doubt she could save it. She hadn't even been told what exactly one did to be married until the day they married and went to stay the night at the house of Guy Ed and Betty Sloan. Betty had taken her aside and told her what happened and that she should make sure she greased herself with Vaseline or it would hurt. Then Guy Ed and Betty went out for a night of pitch at friends' leaving the house to the newlyweds so they could become husband and wife in body as well as spirit.

Little Jewel lay there next to her husband thinking what have I done. Her husband put his left arm around her and she lifted her head to rest on it. Then he took her right hand in his and put it on his thing that she didn't know the name of. It was much larger and much harder than she had imagined. He said can we do it now and she said oh dear God that thing won't go in me. He guffawed, and then he leaned up on his arms to look at her in the glow of the kerosene lamp. He said I don't want to hurt you ever. He said why don't I just kiss you why we haven't even had a kiss. And when his soft lips covered her mouth, she really would have fallen if she had not been in bed already. He kissed her until she wanted something more. Then he lay on top of her, on top of the sheet until she pulled the sheet out from between them. She felt blood rush to the spot where they would be joined, she thought I've forgot to put on Vaseline. He reached down and slid up her gown, he slid his hand to the top of her underwear and said do you care if we take these off?

Please do she said.

Little Jewel moved the jar of roses, frozen and dried by the January freeze, roses the girls had placed there over Christmas—that Sharon had brought with her from the Rio Grande valley. Sharon was their flower daughter, the one who should have been named Rose.

Little Jewel began to dig into the red clay. All those years she had thought he came back for one reason—she had staked everything on his passion for her, the kind that she had felt for him. She had staked everything on blind faith, that if given a choice—the other woman, or her—and given the message that she would in no way share him, he would choose her. And she thought that's what had happened. She never saw the other woman who, so she had been told, finding herself alone had moved to Texas to be near her family. After a while she'd forgotten about her, almost.

To insure that the stakes were simply woman against woman, Little Jewel had not told him she was with child, and she had made it clear to him the day she packed and moved to Cora Emery's she would never forbid him to see their children at any time, that she would never ask him for a thing, and that she would even vote for him for sheriff—which had made him laugh in spite of the seriousness of the conversation.

She had prayed fervently of course, but not for his return. She had simply prayed for the strength to stick to her demand.

That night around the Christmas tree, when she heard the truth—or *a* truth that belied her own—she swallowed her shock like bitters and said to herself you must forget you heard this. She forgot it through the whole of Christmas, she forgot it through the storm as she waited to hear that her children had all made it safely back to their own homes. She was so successful at forgetting that she forgot it through the basketball tournament when she helped out, as always, at the school kitchen.

Then it was February and their anniversary so

she could no longer forget, no longer forget that David Ben might, after all, have come back to her because of duty, or because he could not bear to be shut off from his mother or sisters, or daughters.

Little Jewel stopped digging at her husband's grave and walked up the slope where the bodies of Montgomery and J. D. Sugars rested—a few graves removed from Jacob Sugars who had come here in 1815, had come from Tennessee with seeds and slaves, had come with his wife, Zenobia, who was rumored to be full-blooded Cherokee, with his twelve-year-old son Benjamin David, had come and found the spring that gave clear, sweet water.

Since J. D. Sugars' brother had produced no offspring, the last of the Sugars line had died with her David Ben, causing her to lament, almost, that she didn't have a son, but she was so grateful for having six healthy children that she didn't dare let such a thought linger.

She looked to the northeast edge of the cemetery and saw that the Rose of Sharon bush shading Cora Emery McRae's grave some distance from theirs needed cutting back. She had promised Cora Emery she'd see to it that she got the spot next to her husband, James McRae, whose grave was just out of the shade of the black cherry tree. She'd lived up to that promise even though she had to argue hard and long with the cemetery committee since Horace Higginbottom, ex-principal, ex-superintendent and at that time the president of the school board, had claimed that spot for himself.

Little Jewel suspected it wasn't only her persuasion that caused Horace to change his mind. She suspected Montgomery had gone to Horace convincing him to relinquish his claim on that spot for himself since it was near his mother by threatening to tell the world that Horace Higginbottom had tried to force his affection on her war-widowed daughter when his wife was away at a PTA convention.

She looked back to Montgomery's grave, which had a bigger tombstone than Montgomery would have wanted, but Little Jewel couldn't restrain herself when she went to pick it out and she convinced the daughters that their mama deserved a finer marker than she would have chosen for herself.

There had been a simple graveside service for Montgomery. On her deathbed she had said if y'all make a production of my death I'll kick your damn asses—every one of you. She said Jewel I'm countin' on you to make them keep their goddamn word.

Little Jewel had hardly heard Montgomery utter a sentence without a swear word sneaking in somewhere, even though Montgomery took her hand to her girls—when they were girls—if they tried to imitate her. She had, of course, never taken her hand to her son, but having his father's temperament, he had never acquired the habit anyway—or at least not in the company of women.

And Montgomery never broke the habit. The

last thing she said was, is it me or is it too goddamn hot in here.

Once when Jewel and the sisters and Montgomery were in the Sugars kitchen cooking fish for a horde of people, the war-widowed daughter with lavender eyes was talking about what attracted a woman. She said Mama what did Daddy have when he was only fifteen years old that made you want to marry him, why he'd have still been a fuzzy-faced boy.

Montgomery without even a slight pause said I wanted to get away from home, from my mama and papa and brothers and sister—all of them trying to make me talk proper like a lady. I just didn't hanker to be a lady. Now don't get me wrong, I did have a hankering for your papa, but mostly I had to be free to cuss all I wanted.

Little Jewel laughed. She looked at Montgomery Sugars' headstone. Then Little Jewel Flowers Sugars did something she'd never done in her life. She said damn.

It came out as a whisper but she had said it. Then she said it a bit louder. Damn. Then even louder. *Damn.*

That afternoon at Junior Gilbert's store, Tucker Martin swore that he'd driven by the cemetery that morning and seen Little Jewel Sugars beating Montgomery Sugars' gravestone with a shovel and cussin' like a sailor. They said come on now Tucker, they said in her sixty-five or so years Little Jewel had never cussed, they said the closest she'd get to a swear would be to say I'll swan. They said Little Jewel has never put her hand to anyone, except a swat to a misbehaving child maybe. They said what you saw musta been Little Jewel packin' down the azaleas she was puttin' in. But Tucker swore she was beating Montgomery's grave for all she was worth.

Of course no one believed Tucker Martin, blaming it on the failing eyesight of age. Nor would they have believed anyone who might have ventured closer that day and would have been willing to swear on a stack of Bibles that Little Jewel Flowers Sugars stood there yelling at a tombstone, flailing a shovel on top of a grave and screaming at the top of her voice damn you Miz Montgomery, damn you damn you. Damn you to almighty Hell and back.

6

The Salvation of Cora Emery McRae

He that believeth and is baptized shall be saved; He that believeth not shall be damned.

Mark 16:16

1951

Cora Emery McRae sat on the second row of the Sugars Spring, Arkansas, Baptist Church listening to the Reverend Lucas Tanner's closing sermon of the spring revival and wondering how in Heaven's name she finally let Little Jewel Sugars talk her into attending church. It was Cora Emery's seventy-second birthday and she would much rather be commemorating it at the Farm Bureau fish fry at Hope, or even at home where she could have sat on her porch watching the last light of day before retiring inside to listen to the Louisiana Hayride. Bob Wills and his Texas Playboys were the special guests and she hadn't wanted to miss that.

But back in January, Cora Emery had made the mistake of promising Little Jewel she'd attend the summer revival at least one night. It had seemed at the time that the jaws of winter would forever hold spring at bay. Besides, Little Jewel had eased the suggestion into their conversation ever so gently as she helped Cora Emery lug a tow sack of grain to her feed shed and before Cora Emery could bite her tongue, she had said well yes I'll go with you just one night since it means so much to you.

One thing folks in Sugars Spring knew about Cora Emery McRae—the Yankee woman who had arrived there a stranger to one and all fifty-one years ago, the woman they still called Cora Emery as if it were her given name—was that she honored her promises.

Little Jewel had stopped by every day of the revival saying Miz Cora Emery is this the night you're gonna come with me to church and Cora Emery had said she didn't think she was up to it. But today, on the very last day when Little Jewel appeared holding a white cake tin and a quart Ball jar of sweet ice tea, Cora Emery had sighed in surrender.

Little Jewel Sugars might have been the gentlest of women but she was dogged when she set her mind to something, probably as dogged as any woman Cora Emery had known, except maybe Phoenicia Standfry, who, somewhere in her eighties, got it in her head that she should learn how to drive and insisted that Cora Emery teach her.

So folks in Bethel and Sugars Spring who happened to be passing by would see Cora Emery's De Soto out in her pasture lurching in zigs and zags and circles around her patch of persimmons, and her steers. Everyone in Bethel and Sugars Spring laughed and scratched their heads at the spectacle, and Cora Emery found herself thinking if Phoenicia keeps insisting on these drives, she's gonna drive me to praying.

But Phoenicia, the last of those friends, was no longer living, so—Cora Emery concluded as she tried not to think about how hard the pine benches were—Little Jewel Sugars was now the most stubborn creature living with the exception of Herbert, Cora Emery's mule. And of course with the exception of Montgomery Sugars, who had let it be known to Little Jewel in no uncertain terms that she was going to end her days a slipped-away Methodist and there wasn't a goddamn thing Little Jewel could do about it. With that thought, a two-syllable chuckle escaped Cora Emery at the very moment the minister asked *do you have any earthly notion how truly horrifying the judgment day is going to be?*

The chuckle, to be sure, was hardly loud enough to be detected in normal circumstances, but in the church building it magnified itself traveling backward several rows, and traveling forward to the podium, startling the minister precisely as he rephrased his question *can you conceive how awful it will be to burn in Hell* causing Preacher Tanner to stop in the middle of his question mark and look at her the way she had looked at a disobedient child when she had been a teacher.

Lucas Tanner took a deep breath and was set to resume his sermon when Cora Emery said I surely do beg your humble pardon, I wasn't laughing about Hell. She was about to add I was laughing about how Little Jewel here is as stubborn as my old mule Herbert, why it's taken her thirty-one years to get me to darken the doors of this church. Then Cora Emery thought about asking the reverend if he thought Hell, or Heaven even, was someplace other than this earth, even though she recognized the nature of the question as one nobody is expected to answer, because the answer lies in the awesomeness of the question. One of those questions like when her James died and she looked at the sky and said whatever am I going to do.

But Cora Emery wasn't given to overexplain—which folks in Sugars Spring had long since written off as a Yankee oddity—so she stopped with her simple declaration. Little Jewel placed her left hand over Cora Emery's right one giving it a tender squeeze. Lucas Tanner straightened his tie and resumed his sermon. Cora Emery, deciding one good thing about church is that it gives you time to think, that is if you just don't let the preacher interrupt too much, wandered away to other birthdays. Her sixth: when she got her slate and pencils and a child's rolltop desk. Her fifteenth: the moonlight hayride along Crooked River near her home in Maine and her first kiss from Forrest Twitchell—or was it George Miller—how could she have forgotten which? No matter. She hadn't forgotten the sweet smell of the hay. For her tenth, her grandfather had traveled to Vermont for precisely the right horse—a Morgan—boarding it at the neighbors' for a fortnight to keep it secret.

On the morning of that birthday, her mother had come into her room, tied back the damask curtains letting the sun throw yellow squares across the wide heart-pine floors, and said for her to look outside. Cora, eyes matted with sleep, stumbled over to the window, not yet remembering she was at last ten years old. She looked out to see her grandfather trotting up the lane on the back of a bay, the bay's auburn coat gleaming in the yellow sunlight. Cora thought at the time—and still thought to this day—the Morgan bay was the most magnificent creature that would ever grace the earth. She named him Thor after the Norse god she read about in her grandfather's library.

Cora Emery closed her eyes to watch Thor and a young girl bounding down a packed dirt road, his tail lifted high and switching, the girl's flaxen hair bouncing in rhythm, the early sun causing the dew to flicker like fireflies. Little Jewel, mistaking Cora Emery's daydreaming for dozing, squeezed her hand again and leaned close enough to jostle her shoulder.

And do you have any idea how many tears Jesus has shed for you the preacher was saying as Cora Emery opened her eyes for Little Jewel's sake. The idea of counting tears was so ridiculous she decided not to ponder it at all. She had never been much for crying, and she had used the last of her tears when her James died in 1916. She hadn't cried the one time Thor had thrown her in a battle of wills when he wanted to turn for home and she insisted on going farther. She'd wanted to cry when her grandfather washed the bits of gravel from her skinned and bleeding hands with alcohol, but she didn't want him to think he'd given her the horse when she was too young, since she was only ten and he'd always told her she had to wait until she was twelve to get a horse, so Cora had clamped her jaws, blocked back the tears and said it doesn't smart too bad.

Her grandfather had known he wouldn't live to see her mark her twelfth year. But Cora the child hadn't understood that. That understanding had come only lately when she'd begun to be visited by her own death. It wasn't that Cora Emery felt peaked, she still felt hearty most of the time. She wasn't in pain, even at those moments when she knew death was circling her, staking its claim. Mostly, at those moments, what she felt was a shortness of breath, and a certain weightlessness, a certain separation from everything around her. That feeling came at unpredictable moments—at the kitchen sink with her hands deep in hot sudsy water, or in the garden where Cora still got on her knees and pulled weeds even though Little Jewel was always saying I'll swan Miz Cora Emery, you're taxin' yourself too much, please let me find someone to do your weeding for you. And Cora Emery would say if I can't do my garden then I won't have a garden. Then Little Jewel would say but I worry that you won't be able to pull yourself up someday. And Cora Emery would say then I can't think of a better place to die than in a mess of flowers. And Little Jewel realizing she was fighting a losing battle would smile and say well I guess if that happened, we could just have your funeral there and save the florists the trouble.

Cora Emery noticed Little Jewel had taken to driving by even more often during weeding time. Insisting she needed the exercise, Little Jewel would bend, tuck the skirt of her cotton dress behind her knees and begin pulling up the stubborn Johnson grass invading Cora Emery's flower bed.

If Cora Emery didn't love Little Jewel almost like a daughter, she loved her more than she loved anyone else. She'd decided she loved Little Jewel when Jewel Flowers was twelve years old, at a time when Cora Emery's entire life seemed to be covered by a storm cloud.

Cora Emery had watched Little Jewel tending the sick at the makeshift hospital at this very church after the cyclone of 1920 hit the outskirts of Bethel, where the coloreds live and which the whites always called Chickenham, then turned its wrath on Sugars Spring, taking the lives of eight people, twenty-seven cows, one bull, eleven pigs, and Lord knows how many chickens. It sliced roofs off barns and chicken sheds and toolhouses, and totally devoured six houses, Cora Emery's included.

At the time, Cora Emery was walking Rebekah Sarah Weaver, the old, old colored woman to her home in Bethel when Rebekah Sarah, who claimed the gift and curse of visions, told Cora Emery that the cloud, violet and lined with green, would consume Cora's house, but that they would not be harmed. She had even told Cora Emery who it would kill—Rebekah Sarah's granddaughter among them—and that Isannah Sanders would hurl through the air.

Sure enough, when Cora Emery returned home, all that was left of the house James had built for them was a patch of brown the color of burlap. And her front steps, which hadn't budged.

The Sugars Spring Baptist Church became a hospital—as the Church of Christ hadn't yet raised enough money for their own building and met at the home of Lottie and Milton Ellis and the Methodist church had disappeared except for the benches that were, unfathomably, still in rows—and Cora Emery, as did many of the women of the village, spent the following days at the church tending the injured.

Little Jewel Flowers even as young as she was hadn't flinched from anything. It was Little Jewel and Cora Emery who helped Doc Walker perform the most unsightly tasks—sewing up the large gaps in skin, digging deeply embedded splinters of wood, glass and straw from a person's body. When women fainted at the sight, or became nauseated from the smell, Little Jewel, a small-framed girl, looking even younger with her unruly black hair swirling around a round, pale face, stepped in and took their places.

One day, she and Little Jewel were resting for a spell under the catawba tree behind the church and eating fried pies folks in White Bluff had sent with the mail carrier. Little Jewel said Miz Cora Emery, I went by your place yesterday and I'll swan, that cloud sure did chew up your house didn't it.

Cora Emery smiled at Little Jewel's manner, at her wide-eyed and almost joyful astonishment at the power of the storm, and she said it sure did child, and Little Jewel said why I declare it didn't even leave enough to pick your teeth with.

Cora Emery started laughing. First a chuckle, then a ripple, then she was on the ground guffawing, holding a fried dried-apple pie in one hand and her aching sides on the other. Little Jewel was horrified at first because she had no earthly idea what had possessed Cora Emery, since Cora Emery was known as no-nonsense and not one given to expression, but as Little Jewel's father was such a taciturn man who allowed no festivities and little laughter in their house, Little Jewel, deciding not to question Cora Emery's outburst even though she had no idea what the Yankee woman was laughing at, took every advantage to revel in it.

So, anyone who happened around back of the church that day would have seen a stout woman already past forty, and a slight, gangly girl of twelve whooping and rolling and holding their sides like they were at a vaudeville show instead of a hospital that was also a house of God.

That was when Cora Emery began to love Little Jewel Flowers who four years later, at age sixteen, snatched the town's most eligible bachelor—from hands and hearts of girls ten times prettier—to become Little Jewel Sugars.

And whose fault is it, when those in your own community pass away outside the state of grace, just who do you think God will hold accountable, especially if you haven't done all in your power to open their eyes, to sharpen their hearing. Jesus, himself, told us about these folks in Matthew thirteen-fifteen, he said their hearts are waxed gross, their ears are dull of hearing, and their eyes have closed.

Cora Emery knew Little Jewel had long since felt accountable for her soul even though she had said to her time and time again Little Jewel, you've done all you can, you've almost nagged me to death so no god in his right mind would hold it against you. And Little Jewel would say but I love you Miz Cora Emery and I loved Mr. James and I don't want you two to be separated in the hereafter.

James. Could it really have been fifty-one years since she met James? Could it really have been fifty-one years since she waved good-bye to her parents and set off to return the items that had lain in her grandfather's desk drawer for thirty-seven years? Had lain there since 1863.

Sometimes, Cora Emery thinks that if she got on a train today, her mother and father would be waiting at the station. She thinks maybe it's because she didn't get to be at their funerals—both of them dying of an outbreak of influenza—that she thinks of them still living, staying the age they were when she left. But sometimes she imagines her grandfather waiting there too, even though she saw his body lowered into the ground.

Two months before Cora's twelfth birthday, her grandfather had died of a heart attack as he dismounted Big Gray in front of the Buckfield General Store. All the town turned out for the funeral and for Cora, at twelve, it had been a dark and wonderful occasion. Her beloved grandfather was gone but she reveled in hearing the speeches, in hearing over and over how he had been so upstanding, a wise man, a good man. A man of his word.

The next day her father, uncles, aunts, mother and the grandchildren began the task of sorting through his big rambling house in the village. Cora had been assigned the task of listing everything in one of the rooms in the attic. It was there she came upon a brown paper bundle. In the same drawer as the package was a packet of letters—all addressed with her grandfather's handwriting. One was *to a Mrs. MacFee, Dooley's Landing, Arkansas.* The return in a tiny, tight handwriting said *no such person lives here.* Another, *to the mother of a J. R. MacFee, deceased the spring of 1863, Dooley's Landing, Arkansas.* That one was returned with bold circular handwriting *no MacFee living or dead.* Letter after letter—all of them returned unopened with similar remarks, some of them helpful in tone, others snipping.

The letters were returned from towns called Hope, Blevins, Spring Hill, Fulton, Columbus. There was a letter from the sheriff of Hampstead County—obviously in answer to one her grandfather had sent—saying that there was no Dooley's Landing anymore since the new railroad had bypassed it, that only a few houses remained and no MacFees lived there, in fact there hadn't been any MacFees so how could a MacFee who didn't exist get killed in the war? The sheriff asked what business did a Yankee have sending something to a Confederate soldier anyway. Cora read that, looked at the heading to see the date—October 1878. It took her by surprise that it was so long after the war. Her grandfather had been trying to return the package for fourteen years. And the sheriff was obviously still bitter for that long as well.

Cora knew she should wait for grown-ups to give permission to open the package, but realizing her grandfather had spent years trying to return it to anyone who might be related to a J. R. MacFee who once lived in a used-to-be place called Dooley's Landing, Arkansas—which to Cora seemed as far away as the moon—she couldn't resist the temptation.

Inside was a man's watch and a man's ring with the initials JRM swirled into it. Cora, sensing she'd found something important, swallowed her dread of the reprimand she'd surely receive for opening something sealed, and showed the letters to her parents. Her father said so that's where that's been all these years. Her mother said I wondered if he ever located that young man's folks.

It was then Cora learned that her grandfather, who had served as a captain under General Steele, had somehow promised a dying Confederate soldier that he'd return those things to his mother. He had spent years trying to do so, then having no luck, put it aside until such time as he could make the journey himself. But each time her grandfather was set to go, something happened. Either an illness, or, being a judge, he might have to settle land disputes between neighbors, or fine someone if they got drunk and rowdy. He had, Cora learned, been packed to go when Cora's grandmother took sick and was bedridden for months. Once he even began the journey, but the train derailed just outside of Boston, breaking his left leg. When Cora heard that, she realized that's why her grandfather had limped ever so slightly—she had always assumed he had fallen from a horse.

At twelve, Cora found herself smitten with the saga of the watch and the ring—smitten with her grandfather's quest to return them. She imagined her grandfather dressed like one of King Arthur's knights, knocking the evil knight standing in his way off of his horse, or she imagined that once her grandfather had been on his way to this place called Arkansas when he was set upon by Jesse James and his gang. She imagined a scruffy outlaw searching her grandfather and when he found the ring and watch her grandfather said shoot me and pull my gold teeth right out of my mouth, but don't take these, it's for the mother of a young Confederate who died in my arms. And Jesse would be so touched he'd almost cry and he'd say let him be boys. (Cora had read much about Jesse James's life and death and she knew Jesse had put much store in his mother, and in the Confederacy.) After a few months the fascination with the saga of the watch and the ring slid to the back of Cora's mind and she went on with the business of growing into womanhood.

Then one evening when she was fifteen or sixteen, she and her mother reminisced about her grandfather and his sense of duty and rightness which was why he had gone to war, and her mother said your grandfather was a man of honor right up to the moment he took his last breath. Her mother went to her desk and took out a sheet of his stationery with a list he'd made the very day he died. A list of things to do before winter: *replace window in hallway, contract Ross to build extension on shed, hire Summers boys to stack wood, fetch hay. Purchase underwear—woolen, storm boots.* He'd listed under *buy* the page number and price of several items from the Sears, Roebuck catalog which promised to be the cheapest supply house on earth. At the bottom of the list and underlined *buy ticket to Arkansas, try town of Sugars Spring.* It was at that moment that Cora made a promise to her grandfather.

Paul didn't say for us to be baptized and then go home and forget about it. He said for us to go into the world to preach the gospel to the Jew first, but also to the Greek. But he didn't mean to go everywhere in the world and forget about your neighborhood, now did he.

Cora blinked her eyes back to the present and waited for someone to pipe in saying tell us Brother Tanner tell us or saying nosirree he didn't mean that, or saying amens the way coloreds did the time she had visited church with her friends in Bethel who had once thought to save her soul as well. Instead, these white Baptists sat stone-faced or nodded their heads ever so slightly. It was a lot easier for a mind to wander in white churches.

There had been much to learn when she arrived in Arkansas in the fall of 1900, a young school-teacher twenty-one years old, carrying out the promise she had made to her deceased grandfather the night her mother showed her that list. She had, of course, gone about her life, finishing high school, flirting with the idea of marriage but finding she lacked adequate interest in any of the prospects, then going to a teachers' college and returning to Buckfield to teach the younger grades in the same school she had attended, the same school her mother had taught for years until she married Cora's father, a seaman who had wandered inland for a visit to relatives. Cora, being what her mother called a change of life baby and what all her family called a blessing, had been the only seed of that marriage.

On the day she turned twenty-one, she came into her share of her grandfather's estate, a modest amount by some standards, enough to make her wealthy by others. Enough, anyway, to finance a trip to Arkansas, and when she returned there should be money left to purchase and build on a piece of land near Streaked Mountain she'd always had an eye on.

She left for Arkansas late that fall, in time to

miss the onset of another New England winter. Her parents did not attempt to talk her out of the journey, even though her mother's eyes glistened and her father's jaw sagged as they hugged her good-bye and she boarded the train in Portland. She told them she would be back in a few weeks. Cora Emery believed they sensed it was the last time they would ever see their only child. It was years later before she understood the pain they carried in their hearts that crisp fall day.

And do you have any idea all the riff-raff that will be your neighbor in Hell? There'll be all the robbers and murderers who ever lived. So your next door neighbor just might be Herod, or Pontius Pilate. Or Jezebel. Or General Sherman.

Or John Wilkes Booth, Cora Emery thought about saying. She put her hand to her mouth to repress a chuckle at the wicked thought and stayed quiet—for Little Jewel's sake.

Now that's the awful part about Hell, but it's not the sad part, my brothers and sisters. They'll be everyday folks there, folks who don't kill, steal from their neighbors, or rob banks, but folks you run into every day at the post office, on the street, in Gilbert's Store, folks who have simply gone asleep and let Satan harden their hearts. Folks who even come to church time after time and never answer the call, never open their hearts and let Jesus in.

Lucas Tanner, mustering what must have been his best look of despair, pulled his handkerchief from his shirt pocket and wiped his brow. *That, my dear, dear Christian friends, is what is* sad, *that is what is* heartbreaking *about Hell.*

Little Jewel nodded her head in heartfelt agreement. Cora Emery shifted on the hard bench and—in what she intended as a whisper to Little Jewel—said I bet the benches in Hell aren't any harder than these. Little Jewel kept her eyes on the preacher and didn't acknowledge Cora Emery's comment. Still, Cora Emery felt the bench vibrate and she knew Little Jewel was trying not to erupt in laughter.

Reverend Lucas Tanner looked at Cora Emery and said *no ma'am they don't even have benches in Hell, no one gets to sit in Hell. And I'd wager they don't have ice tea or lemonade down there either.*

Cora Emery thought he must have the hearing of a bird dog. And even though it was a white Baptist church, a low rumble of laughter gave Little Jewel the chance to release her own. Cora Emery thought Lucas Tanner was pretty sharp to come back with that. He might be okay after all.

Cora Emery never did know how her grandfather had discovered the MacFees might be found in Sugars Spring. When she arrived there, taking a carriage from Hope, a carriage owned and driven by a colored man, the first colored person Cora had ever spoken too, she went directly to the post office only to be told no MacFees had ever lived in Sugars Spring. As she went out the door one of the women said she sure ain't from around here why listen to the way she talks.

Cora then went to Gilbert's General Store where old men sitting on benches or on big roots of the magnolia tree and one of them on a barrel told her the same thing. She told them how this soldier was young and how he had been killed in battle. They shook their heads and named the ones who had died in the war and no name was close to MacFee.

Cora turned to go, feeling her shoulders sag in defeat. Nothing to do but head back to Hope, catch a train back home. She had taken her grandfather's promise as far as she could take it. Hadn't she?

Still, something tickling the back of her mind wouldn't let her leave without one more try. She turned back to the whittlers on the porch, pulled the ring and the watch from her drawstring purse. She said it's just that during the war my grandfather promised to return these she said. She held the watch in one hand, the ring in the other. They all shook their heads as if to say we can't help you lady, so she turned to go, feeling the heaviness in her shoulders even more.

She'd taken only a few steps when she heard a raspy voice say let me see that there ring. Cora Emery turned and the outreached hand of the old man sitting on the barrel, a man who reminded her of the dried-apple dolls her mother had made for her and her cousins every fall.

She placed the ring in his shaking and shriveled hand. The old man took the ring like it was fine crystal, held it close to his dried-apple face, held it away from him to get a better look and said well that solves it, this here ain't a MacFee ring, this here's a McRae ring. It was passed from Uncle Chester to his son, Tag, who went and lost it in battle. But Tag ain't dead a'tall.

Cora Emery asked him if he was sure, meaning about the ring and he said well if he did die we been playing checkers with a ghost for all these years. The men had a good chuckle at that thought and went back to their whittling.

And even though the Holy Bible tells us they ain't gonna be no marriage nor given in marriage in Heaven, that don't mean we won't recognize each other and love each other if we are man and wife on this earth. Those of you in the audience who haven't yet given yourself to Christ but whose spouses are saved already, how you gonna feel standin' here watching them ascend to Heaven while you have to descend into Hell? Think about that. Do you want to spend eternity without your husband or wife?

Cora Emery knew folks in that audience who could in all honesty answer yes to that question so it was just as well it was one of those no-answer-expected questions. She, though, wasn't one of them. In two weeks and four days it would be thirty-five years to the day since James died at the well. That had already been an eternity.

Cora's parents and their parents before them were Unitarian—a belief completely out of range of the imagination of anyone in Sugars Spring. But her faith or lack of it hadn't bothered James, or if it did, he never gave her any indication.

James hadn't been much of a churchgoer but he was a member of this very church and they considered him saved for certain, since forsaking a life of his own, he had taken care of his parents—his father frail from his wounds, his mother thin and delicate, always. Nosirree, there was no question in their minds as to where James McRae was headed.

When Cora took the items to the McRae house, a man she judged to be about twenty-five, even though it turned out he was thirty-five, answered the door. Maybe it was the way the light came from behind her back causing the man to be partly in sun, partly in shadow, or maybe it was the directness with which his dusty brown eyes drank in this young woman standing before him overdressed for Arkansas winters in a wool mackintosh cape trimmed in velvet, or maybe it was how quickly he smiled, or maybe it was the fact that he seemed in no hurry for either of them to say anything that made Cora forget for a minute why she had called. The first words he uttered were well, goodness, what good deed did I do to deserve a visit from an angel.

Later, when they were married, she'd chastise him for his forwardness saying I could have been married and he'd say I couldn't help it, the minute I opened that door I knew my prayers had been answered.

When she did recover from such a bold remark to explain her reason for appearing on his porch, James introduced himself, invited her inside to meet his father who was called Tag all his life but whose name was James Robert, and who was frail but obviously not dead. James talked Cora into staying for supper and then into staying at the boarding house for a few days, then into finishing out the school year for the teacher who had eloped with a traveling shoe salesman, and then, in 1901, he talked her into staying for their lifetime. And since she had been the schoolteacher for the months of their courtship he called her Miz Cora Emery, and he dropped only the Miz part when they got married.

When Cora showed Tag McRae the ring and the watch, he reached back into his memory, dusted off his story and relished in the telling of it—now that it had an ending. Tag fought for General Price and was felled at the edge of a creek, shot in the chest in a skirmish with General Steele's men. When Tag saw his own blood turning the creek water crimson, he was sure he was going to die, so he closed his eyes and tried to picture Dooley's Landing. He saw his mama walking from the barn, milk pails in both hands. He saw her building the fire under the wash pot. He saw her standing on the porch ringing the supper bell. He heard the bell as clear and real as if he were in the barnyard instead of dying at the edge of a creek far away. He heard the sounds of locusts in the elm trees at Dooley's Landing. He heard someone say my God it's just a boy. He opened his eyes and saw a tall man in a Yankee uniform, rifle in hand, looming over him. Tag closed his eyes and waited for the death blow. He remembered or thought he remembered wondering if you heard the sound of the shot that killed you.

After a few seconds when Tag realized he was still breathing, he opened his eyes to see the Yankee bending to him. Tag would have swore he saw tears in the Yankee's eyes. Can I do anything for you son the Yankee said and Tag said yessir I'm dyin' and I want my mama to have my watch. Anything else, the Yankee asked, and Tag said and my ring.

And the Yankee took the tokens of J. R. McRae's life and said I'll do my best to get them to her if you'll give me your name and tell me where to send them. As the people from the hospital wagon picking up the wounded lifted Tag gently into the wagon, he tried to tell his name in what he was sure was his last breath. The last thing Tag remembered was four other soldiers, all of them likewise on the brink of death, being piled on top of him.

But Tag McRae hadn't died like he was supposed to, even though he remained troubled in his
health for the rest of his life. He arrived home to his
family many weeks later, fully expecting—as
strange as it seemed—the ring and the watch to be
there. And when Cora Emery finally placed them in
his hands thirty-seven years later, he said I coulda
sworn that man was someone I could trust even if
he was wearing a Yankee uniform—and after all
these years I been proved right.

*Just think of it, those of you who have not yet
opened your heart to Christ, think of the pleasures
being offered you, not only in Heaven but on this
earth—the pleasures of living as a child of God, in a
state of eternal grace. Think of having Je-sus beside
you through all your trials and tribulations.*

Cora Emery was sure she wouldn't have felt
one bit better if Jesus had been hanging around her
when her son died. Or when her daughter came into
the world without breath that same month. Or
when her parents died that same winter. Or when
James—seemingly vibrant—fell dead at the well
nine years later, on Lottie Ellis's fiftieth birthday.
Because she would have also had Him to blame. At
least this way, Cora Emery had been able to lay it to
the fickleness of nature, to the plain and simple un-
fairness of life.

*Don't, I pray, let one more night pass without
opening your heart to Him. I beg of you. Those who
love you beg of you. Jesus Himself begs of you "ye
who are weary and are heavy laden come and I will*

*give you rest." Please answer His plea as we sing the
song of invitation. Please step out into the aisle, I'll
meet you halfway. Jesus will meet you halfway.
Please, won't you come—as we stand and sing the
song of invitation on page one hundred and twenty-
three of your songbooks.*

Reverend Lucas Tanner spread out his arms in
welcome. Abigail Huff, who had sat straight as a
ruler at the piano the length of the sermon—even
though she was seventy-five—spread out her long
knotted fingers on the piano keys and began playing. Little Jewel took Cora Emery by the elbow to
help her stand as the congregation rose and sang
*softly and tenderly Jesus is calling, calling for you
and for me. See on the portals He's waiting and
watching . . .*

Cora Emery hadn't thought to bring her reading glasses so she couldn't see the words in the hym-
nal that Little Jewel held in front of them. Little
Jewel obviously didn't need the book because she
had her eyes closed, *praying* the song. *Come home.
Come ho-o-ome. Ye who are weary come ho-o-
ome.* Cora Emery knew what dear, sweet Little
Jewel Sugars was praying for all right, she was praying for the soul of Cora Emery, praying for her to
walk down the aisle and be born again.

Cora Emery, though, had no intention of being
born again. Once was enough. She stood there hoping no one would walk down the aisle so they'd just
be done and she could get home in time to hear the
tail end of the Louisiana Hayride.

Earnestly, tenderly Jesus is calling. Calling oh sinner, come home . . .

To Cora Emery's displeasure, several people came walking down the aisle. Even Whitey Mott—noted for burying pints of moonshine under his wife's rosebushes. Each time someone stepped into the aisle the Reverend Lucas Tanner scurried down to meet them, putting his arm around them and leading them to the front row, where he sat them, gave them a pat or two and then stood back and looked for who else might be touched by the spirit.

Cora Emery didn't like to think she was cold-spirited, but mostly she was thinking about missing her radio show. She hadn't even liked the music of this land at first. But James had loved it. Course he died before they had a radio. She closed her eyes and saw James sitting beside her on the porch swing patting his foot to a song he's singing. His eyes meet hers and he reaches over to put his arm around her.

Cora Emery opened her eyes to meet his. Instead, it is Little Jewel's eyes looking into hers, Little Jewel who, thinking Cora Emery's eyes are closed in prayer, has put her arms around her for comfort. *Time is now fleeting, the moments are passing, passing from you and from me* . . . Cora Emery closes her eyes just in case James is still there.

Shadows are gathering, deathbeds are coming, coming for you and for me . . . And he is. James is still there, sitting on the porch rocker singing "Jimmy Crack Corn" while Jimmy, their tow-headed five-year-old, thinking the song had been made up just for him, jumps, dances, leaps, spins in a circle. Cora Emery sits on the swing, knitting a sweater for the child she is expecting in the winter. The song ends and Jimmy stops his spin, staggers for balance and says Mama sing with Poppa. She can't carry a tune in a bucket, but James says yeah, come on Cora Emery sing for us. He grins that grin that would have melted a Maine lake in January. Lord he has a cunning grin.

She smiles in surrender and says let me build a fire in the stove so we won't have to go without supper, then I'll come back out and sing. Cora Emery feels herself lifting with the sheer joy of the moment. Cora Emery puts her knitting beside her on the swing, and rises to go into the kitchen, then suddenly panic strikes her. Cora Emery jerks her head.

Did she forget to turn off the gas under the beans which she'd meant only to parboil? Did she leave the hotpad too close to the burner? Oh heavens. Her house will burn down.

Cora Emery, almost pushing Little Jewel down into her seat in her effort to get by, lunges into the aisle. Lunges into the waiting arms of Reverend Lucas Tanner who's saying welcome home dear sister McRae, welcome home at last.

That's where I'm going, she says, then realizing

he doesn't understand, she shouts I've got to check the stove. But the congregation is singing with such resounding fervor since Cora Emery McRae the Yankee woman has, at long last, seen the light after years and years of gardening during church time on Sunday morning that the minister can't make out a word she's saying.

Reverend Lucas Tanner pulls Cora toward the front row and presses her rigid, resisting form onto the bench, thinking Cora Emery is being born again and the power of the spirit entering her body has practically paralyzed her.

In desperation, Cora Emery turns to Little Jewel who's standing behind her, bending down to enfold her.

I got to get home, I left the stove on under my beans, they'll dry up and explode all over my kitchen she hollers into Little Jewel's ears as the congregation sings yet another verse *come home, come home . . .*

Little Jewel hears, or reads, her lips and yells into her ears don't worry, I'll get David Ben to go check it. Little Jewel is down the aisle in a flash— too quick for Lucas Tanner to assume she has a sin to confess and reach out and grab her the way he snagged Cora Emery who twists her body around and watches Little Jewel talking to her husband, the sheriff, who always sits on the back seat on the pretense of needing to be near the door in case he's called away for sheriff duties. In a flash, Little Jewel is back, standing behind Cora Emery who has turned to the front in sheer exasperation. Little Jewel is holding Cora Emery's shoulders, leaning over and kissing her cheeks, saying loudly in her ears, now you're finally and truly home Miz Cora.

Cora Emery turns around, again, and shouts to Little Jewel and to the whole congregation this is all-fired ridiculous, all I want to do is go home and check my beans. But no one is listening so it's like talking to her shoes.

Then it comes. The quick shallow breathing, her weight draining from her. Cora Emery knows unless she can take deeper, heavier breaths she will float to the ceiling, she will turn to mist, she will float to the brown water-stain circle above her and then dissipate, pass through the ceiling and into sky, into nothingness.

Well, Cora Emery thinks, at least they'll have something to talk about for years at Gilbert's Store. *It was the darndest thing, one second she's on the front row waiting to confess her faith and the next second she's floating above us all and then can you believe she vanished right through the roof. Never saw hide nor hair of her again.* Despite the fix she's found herself in, Cora Emery shakes her head and laughs, laughs out loud. *And can you believe she died laughing.*

With her laugh and the shaking of her head in disbelief at all that's happening, an act interpreted as the receiving of the spirit by the congregation,

Cora feels her weight returning—like warm water pouring into her body, water filling her empty feet, anchoring her to the hardwood floor, water rising through her legs, up her body, down her arms causing them to tingle, warm water flowing gently to her head. Her quick light breath becomes slow, steady and deep.

Little Jewel Sugars' face is once again against Cora Emery's, Little Jewel's tears bathing Cora Emery's face, streaming down Cora Emery's face like they were Cora Emery's own.

Cora Emery breathes in as far as she can and lets the air out in a long, slow sigh. She knows, now, for a reason she can't name, she will stay seated, seated with the others who have come forward—until the congregation sings every single verse at least twice. She'll sit right there and miss Bob Wills, and Kitty Wells too. She'll stay right there with the others until she goes through whatever rituals they'll put them through. At least these are not the hard-shell foot-washing kind of Baptists. She couldn't abide anyone else washing her feet. But they are dunkers, so they'll probably dunk her in the river.

She certainly hopes they don't expect any confession from her, certainly not any naming of her sin. What would she name it anyway? She hadn't been raised to dwell on sin, so she wasn't familiar with its terrain. She had, though, heard her grandfather lecture about the sanctity of law. And she had long wondered, maybe even worried somewhat, that she had not honored that sanctity, having known long before old Phoenicia spilled out her story to her on Phoenicia's porch years later, that Phoenicia and Rebekah Sarah—and Samuel Daniel McElroy—had somehow brought about the unfortunate end of Oliver Ray Spears.

Until Phoenicia's story though, she had thought Samuel Daniel had done the killing and the two old women had kept their silence and woven the stories they told the authorities to protect him—which since he was kin was somewhat understandable.

But why had she, Cora Emery, when David Ben questioned her, chosen not to tell him that she'd seen Samuel Daniel McElroy unhitch Phoenicia and Rebekah Sarah's old mule, what was his name? and then pull something across the field from her house, and that whatever he pulled, he left there.

And to this day, she wonders if Phoenicia was telling her the truth or if Phoenicia had crafted yet another story to remove any charge of murder from Samuel Daniel, in case anyone—Cora Emery took that *anyone* to be referring specifically to herself— who might have seen him that day should somehow develop a loose tongue. After all, Phoenicia told Cora Emery that same day that she was going to be meetin' her Maker any day now, gonna be passin' before the moon came round full she suspected, so there wasn't anything the authorities here on this earth could do to her could they. And she told Cora Emery she knew Baby Girl was never, ever coming back. Would Phoenicia really craft such a tale?

Samuel Daniel McElroy was another story. One she knew she'd never figure out, one that she had wondered about from time to time since the day of the baseball game, those many years ago, wasn't it a sunny April day that he had gotten down from his mule-drawn wagon, stepped up to the home plate made from a flour sack, stepped up as diffident as you please, then looked Buckner Rose in the eye, or was it Red Cummings, yes Red was the pitcher, looked Red in the eye, before proceeding to hit a ball to kingdom come and back again. She wondered if Samuel Daniel McElroy did have a bullet in him like Phoenicia said he did from a fight in Louisiana before he settled down and married the first of his how many wives, some say three, some say four, and now at what—sixty?—he's a deacon in the Bethel Baptist Tabernacle Church.

Did he see her that day? After all she had started across the field to see what had drawn Rebekah Sarah and Phoenicia and now Samuel Daniel into the field, and now she can't remember what stopped her. Probably the rain that started about that time.

Just the other day, she had seen him walking across that same field going down to check on some cattle on land he now owned. She remembered seeing him the day that Baby Girl, who named herself

Jasmine Rose, left town with Wadie White in a trail of red swirls, remembered seeing him walking away from what it was he'd carried there, getting drenched by the rain that poured from the cloud. As drenched as she's going to be when she gets baptized, as drenched as she's going to be if she doesn't come to her senses and walk right out of this church this very minute and go home. She wonders if David Ben got to her house in time to keep the beans from exploding. And what about the hotpad? If her house is now a fiery furnace does she even want to know? She wonders if they'll baptize them this very night, or if they'll wait until tomorrow after regular church, like she knows they sometimes do. She wonders if her feet will stay planted when the minister dips her back into the cold, sweet waters of Clear Creek, a creek fed by Sugars Spring.

Cora Emery closes her eyes and watches a sturdy middle-aged woman with flaxen hair, dulled by strands of gray even though she's just turned forty-one, sitting on steps that aren't attached to anything. A woman just returned home to find a tornado had sucked up her house, leaving nothing but front steps, still in place, steps attached to nothing. Cora Emery sees herself sitting there looking at the patch the color of burlap in place of the house James had built the year they were married. The storm has blown over all her trees but one, and yanked up most all her flower bushes except for the azaleas. The irises are mud-splattered and leaning.

But the jonquils, the most delicate looking of her flowers, are still yellow and bright as baby chicks.

Cora Emery McRae sits there thinking this is the final straw. Her James had passed away in 1916. Nine years before that, late in 1907, her five-year-old son, Jimmy, coughed to death in her arms, the same winter her daughter came into the world without breath, the same winter Little Jewel Flowers came into the world.

All of those times, even the birth of Little Jewel Flowers that January, shortly after Cora Emery and James had buried their newborn daughter next to little James—Cora thought she too would die. She had sometimes hoped she would. But of course, she hadn't. And now her house and all the tokens of her life there are gone.

This is the final straw she says again, first to herself, and then out loud to anyone who might be listening. But the congregation is once more singing the refrain *calling oh sinner come home.*

On those steps that day in 1920, Cora Emery had decided not to return to Maine even though she knew she would always long to, but she also knew that longing to return and returning were not the same thing. At Lottie Ellis's insistence, Cora Emery lived with Lottie and Milton whose house the cyclone in its fickleness had spared, and she built again in the same spot, in between this place called

Sugars Spring, Arkansas, and a place called Bethel, getting help with the framing and the masonry, but doing much of the other work herself. She sawed and hammered and nailed and painted. She planted sweetgum, blackgum, a row of cottonwoods. She put rosebushes where the old ones had been. The persimmons in the pasture had not been touched.

When she dug into the ground to transplant a crepe myrtle bush Lottie Ellis had given her, she found the ring that had brought her to this land. The storm had taken it from one of her sewing machine drawers and buried it in the far corner of her front yard, buried it in the spot where white sand, red clay and rich black soil ran together, buried it in the land that slowly but gradually was laying claim to her.

When she moved into her new house six months after the cyclone, on the thirtieth of September 1920, Little Jewel Sugars, who would soon turn thirteen, was the first visitor, arriving with a shiny face, a crisp dress, and a basket of fried chicken and biscuits and potato salad and baked beans and a Mason jar of ice sun-tea, sweating and sweetened, and dried-peach pie that Jewel had made herself while her parents were at a doctor's appointment in Hope.

Cora Emery sits there on the first row of the Sugars Spring Baptist Church, sits on a bench harder than any steps she's sat on over the years, sits watching a twelve-year-old girl with coal-black flyaway hair dancing around a small round face walking into Cora Emery's new house, loaded down with her offerings, looking around with amazement and saying Miz Cora Emery hasn't the Lord given you a beautiful day to come home.

They decide to eat outside since the sun has chased away the snip of fall mornings and warmed the ground for sitting. Cora Emery McRae, who everyone says is a good moral woman but will die an infidel, and Little Jewel Sugars, who that September morning made a promise to herself and to her God not to let that happen, sit in Cora Emery's yard, partaking of the shade of the sweetgum, the one tree, besides the pasture persimmon trees, on Cora Emery's property that had survived the cyclone, partaking of the feast Little Jewel Flowers has spread before them on homespun cloth.

Partaking of communion.